Carter

Remington Ranch Book Three

Carter and Summer

SJ McCoy

A Sweet N Steamy Romance

Published by Xenion, Inc

Published by Xenion, Inc.
First paperback edition 2016
www.sjmccoy.com

This book is a work of fiction. Names, characters, places, and events
are figments of the author's imagination, fictitious, or are used
fictitiously. Any resemblance to actual events, locales or persons
living or dead is coincidental.

Cover Design by Dana Lamothe of Designs by Dana
Editor: Mitzi Pummer Carroll
Proofreaders: Aileen Blomberg and Kristi Cramer

ISBN 978-1-946220-04-2

Dedication

For Sam. Sometimes, life really is too short. Few x

Chapter One

Carter made his way back to his truck. He was ready to head home. After putting in a long day to get Cassidy's landscaping finished, he wanted to hit the shower and then go hit the gym. He should stop by Beau's rental house before he headed back up the valley, but he couldn't bring himself to do it. He'd been putting it off for a couple of days now. Whenever he stopped by that house, a sense of sadness crept over him. Summer Breese had stayed there for a little while. She was Cassidy's friend. She'd become *his* friend—for a short time. Until that story about them had run in the paper. He sighed and unlocked his truck. It had all been lies, but that hadn't mattered. It had been enough to upset Summer's sister, Autumn. It had been enough to make her return to Nashville to straighten things out. Carter climbed into his truck and sat there for a moment. He knew he was a dumbass, but he'd truly believed that she would come back. She was supposed to, but she hadn't. He shook his head. It was for the best.

He looked up at the sound of a truck approaching. Damn! He should've gotten himself moving while he could. Now Shane and Cassidy were home. He put a smile on his face as Shane's red Tundra pulled up beside him.

"Hey, Big C," called Shane. "Where do you think you're going? You should stay and have dinner with us."

"That's okay, thanks. I'll get out of your hair."

"It's no trouble," said Cassidy with a smile as she came around the truck. "We'd love to have you."

Carter smiled back. Cassidy was so good to him. She seemed to understand him pretty well. "Thanks, but I want to hit the gym."

Shane laughed. "Surely you can skip it for one night?"

"I could, but I don't want to."

"You might want to skip it and stick around for dinner if you knew that Cassidy has some news for you."

Carter's heart began to hammer in his chest. It had to be news about Summer. What other news would Cassidy have to tell him? He gave her an inquiring look.

She nodded. "I talked to Summer this afternoon."

Damn, if he couldn't feel the heat in his cheeks! He was a grown-ass man and here he was blushing like a schoolgirl! At least neither of them teased him. "And?"

"And she's coming back tomorrow."

"Tomorrow?"

Cassidy nodded. "I'm going to pick her up from the airport. Do you want to come?"

He shook his head rapidly.

"Why not, bro?" asked Shane. "I'm sure she'd be thrilled to see you there waiting when she lands."

He shook his head again. "No. It wouldn't be right."

"But…" began Cassidy.

"And besides, I'm working." He watched Shane and Cassidy exchange a look he didn't quite understand.

Cassidy shrugged. "Okay then, but I hope you'll at least come over for dinner tomorrow night?"

He pursed his lips. "I don't think that would be right either. I think the best thing I can do is stay out of her way. I don't want to cause any more trouble for her."

"You won't!" insisted Cassidy. "You didn't cause any in the first place. It was that Angie that went to the newspaper!"

Carter shrugged. "You already know what I think about all that. There wouldn't have been any story or pictures for the newspaper to run, if it weren't for me. I'm best staying out of her way." He looked from Cassidy to Shane. "For *my* sake as well as hers."

Shane nodded sadly. "If that's how you feel."

"It is." Carter smiled. "Thanks, guys. I know you're trying to look out for me, but I think it's best this way. I'm not going to lie about how I feel, but we all know it can't go anywhere."

"But Carter…."

He shook his head at Cassidy. "But nothing. I'm going to head on home."

"Okay," said Shane, "but don't be a stranger."

He smiled at them as he pulled away. How could he not be a stranger if Summer was going to be here? Self-preservation dictated that he had to stay the hell out of her way!

~ ~ ~

Summer pulled the zipper closed on her bag and turned to face her sister. "Are you sure you don't want to come with me for a couple of days? You know Cass would love to see you. I'd love you to see the place where I'm staying, get to know the people there." She hesitated, but decided to say it. "I could introduce you to Carter?"

Autumn shook her head. "Perhaps I'll get up there in a week or two, but I really can't take the time right now." Her face softened as she smiled. "Don't worry, I'm okay with it. I'm over it, all right? I was mad at you because I thought you were going to throw away your career out of fear. I thought you were latching onto a guy and buying a house because you didn't think you were going to get your voice back. If you actually care about him, that's a different matter altogether, isn't it?"

Summer nodded. It *was* a different matter. But it wasn't as simple as Autumn believed it to be either. She *did* care about Carter. She cared about him way more than she should, considering the short time she'd known him. The trouble was, she cared way too much to get involved with him since she didn't know where it could go. The last thing in the world she would want to do was hurt him. His life, his whole world was right there in Paradise Valley. If—and it was a big if—she got her voice back and continued with her singing career, it would mean she'd have to end anything the two of them started.

Autumn put a hand on her shoulder. "Don't look so sad, everything will work out the way it's supposed to. You're not going to figure it all out today. Just relax. Take your three months up there in Montana and enjoy yourself. With any luck, by the end of that time, you'll have your voice back, your career back, and maybe a Carter to bring back to Nashville with you."

Summer gave her a weak smile. She knew that would never happen, though she didn't know how to tell Autumn. She certainly didn't know how to tell her that the way she felt right now, her voice and her career weren't what she wanted most anyway.

Autumn shook her head. "Come on. You're all packed and ready. Let's go out for dinner, have a fun evening. We need to get you to the airport early, and I want to make the most of tonight, since it'll be our last night together for a while."

~ ~ ~

Carter pulled up outside the gym. He wanted to hit the weights hard tonight. It did him good when his mind was as frazzled as it was right now.

He waved when he saw his buddy Travis come out.

"Hey, Carter. You're late tonight."

He nodded. "Yeah, sorry I missed you."

"No worries. I worked with Cody. I'll catch you next time."

"Sure thing." Carter made his way inside. Once he'd dumped his bag in his locker, he went to the row of elliptical machines and chose the one at the very end for his warm-up. He shoved his earbuds in his ears, hoping to block the world out—and block out all the thoughts that were crowding his head. She was coming back. Tomorrow! Of course, the third song that came on his iPod was one of Summer's. He always used to love this song. Before he met her, he envied the guy she was singing about. The guy who filled her every thought, the guy she couldn't wait to see again. For the few weeks she'd been here, he'd allowed himself to imagine that he could be that guy. Since she'd left, he'd swung between wanting to believe that she was singing to him, and hating the guy who she *was* singing to!

He hit the button to skip the song. He was supposed to be trying to take his mind off her. It was too late, though. Just the first few lines had filled his head with memories. He smiled as he thought about the very first time he'd met her in person. He'd managed to avoid her for her first few days in the valley, but then Shane had dragged him over to Cassidy's to get it over with. Cassidy had opened her front door and all Carter had been able to do was smile. He'd shook hands with Summer and hadn't been able to let go. She'd smiled back at him, and held onto his hand, too. She was even smaller and more beautiful in real life than she appeared on TV. And she was even sweeter. Cassidy and Shane had left them alone. Carter had felt completely lost and dumb at first, but Summer had asked him about himself, asked him what he did for a living. He told her about his landscaping and offered to show her what he was working on in Cassidy's yard. Their connection had been instant and obvious—even to him. She smiled at everything he said—no matter how dumb it sounded to him. She looked up at him admiringly when he talked about his work. He'd felt like a jerk when he asked about her career—people must ask her that stuff all the time, but she was so sweet and so gracious. She'd answered all his dumb questions and made him feel as though she wanted him to know, to know her, to know how she felt and what she thought. He shook his head and hit the buttons to increase the resistance on the machine. He was here to work out, not to daydream!

He looked around the gym; it was quiet tonight. Just the usual crowd, working hard, minding their own business. Uh-oh. He dropped his head when he spotted Melanie Barlow. She was a regular, but she wasn't one for working hard—or minding her own business! The last thing he needed was her chattering away at him. She was one of the crowd that hung out with Angie and that Katie. He didn't like them and sure as hell didn't trust them—especially not after the stunt Angie had pulled, going to the local rag with that pack of lies about him and Summer.

He kept his head down, but sighed at the sight of Melanie making her way toward the ellipticals. She climbed on the one beside him with a smile. He was going to have to cut short his warm-up if she tried to make conversation. Of course, she did.

"Hi, Carter. I bet you can't wait to see Summer again."

That brought his head up to look at her, even though he'd just decided to pretend not to hear her. He raised a questioning eyebrow.

She smiled. "Don't look like that. The secret's out that she's coming back tomorrow."

How the hell had the news gotten out? He knew full well that neither Shane nor Cassidy would have said anything to anyone. He shrugged and increased the resistance again.

Melanie looked disappointed, but at least she didn't push for more. Even *she* could observe gym etiquette—to some extent.

When the program finished and his fifteen minutes were up, Carter was grateful that Melanie was slogging through an uphill cycle and couldn't have talked if she wanted to, judging from the way she was sweating and huffing. He made good his escape and headed for the free weights. He knew he'd be safe over there.

He was wrong, though. She followed him.

"So are you two getting back together?" she asked.

"We never were together!" he blurted out, immediately wishing he hadn't spoken at all.

She gave him a coy smile. "It's all right. I'm not Angie. I'm not looking for a story for the papers. I'm just wondering if *I* have a chance."

Carter was so surprised he literally took a step back. "Excuse me?"

She giggled. "Carter, you're quite the catch. Everyone always knew you were off the market…until the whole thing with Summer. If you *are* back in the dating game, and you're really not interested in her, well, I wondered if you and I might go out sometime?"

Carter was lost for words. "I…" He didn't even know how to turn her down politely.

She smiled. "It's okay. You don't have to answer right now. Just think about it and let me know, okay?"

He nodded, which, judging by the smile that spread across her face, might have been the wrong thing to do.

"Great!" She walked away, turning back to give him a little wave before she disappeared into the ladies locker room.

Damn! Did she think he was interested? How the hell had that just happened? He wasn't interested in the least. He *wasn't* back in the dating game. He *didn't* want to go out with her sometime—or anytime! And he *was **really*** interested in Summer! He sat down on the bench and tightened his gloves. What did it matter if he was interested in Summer? It couldn't go anywhere between them. She had a life in Nashville and a career that took her all over the country. He had a career that was his life and his whole world, right here in the valley. Who was he kidding anyway? She was such a sweet person, she'd just been kind to him. She must have known how attracted he was to her; she'd been kind to the big bumbling idiot while she was here. Now she was coming back, she'd probably be relieved not to have to run into him!

~ ~ ~

Summer looked at her watch. The car should be here soon. She couldn't wait to get back to Montana. She was dying to see Cassidy again. To get settled back into the lovely house where she'd been staying. She loved that place! Most of all, she couldn't wait to see Carter. There had been so many times she'd wanted to call him. He was so easy to talk to. She'd wanted to let him know why she hadn't come back yet. She'd wanted to hear his voice! Yet she hadn't called. They were in a difficult situation. They'd developed such a friendship in the time she'd been in the valley. She wanted so much more than that. She believed he did, too. But they'd reached an unspoken agreement. They'd stuck with friendship, not wanting to risk that for the sake of something more, something that, in reality, they both knew they couldn't have.

Her phone buzzed in her purse and she rummaged in the depths for it. It had stopped ringing by the time her fingers closed around it and she pulled it out. She smiled when she saw the name on the display. She called him straight back.

"Summer, darlin', when are you going to learn to keep your phone in your pocket instead of dropping it into that black hole that you call your purse?"

She laughed. "Hi, Clay! Sorry, I didn't get to it in time—and you're absolutely right about why."

Clay's low deep laugh rumbled down the line. "Not a problem, little girl. I just wanted a quick word before you fly out. Wanted to let you know I'll be thinking of you. Anything you need, you call me, you hear?"

She smiled. "Thanks, Clay. I will. You're going to be busy though; the tour starts next weekend, doesn't it?"

"It does, but I'll never be too busy for my favorite little girl. I've got to look after my star signing. I don't want you getting your voice back and going signing with someone else."

"You know I'd never do that!"

He laughed again. "You're right. I do. And I'd sue your little ass if you did!"

She laughed with him. Clay McAdam was one of the biggest country stars there was. He'd signed her to his label a couple of years ago and had become a friend and mentor.

"Seriously though, darlin', while you're hiding out in the mountains, I don't want you to worry. McAdam Records will welcome you back with open arms whenever you're ready. No matter how long it takes."

Summer had to ask the question that had been plaguing her. "What if I don't come back though, Clay? What if I'm never ready?"

There was a long silence before he spoke again. "Why don't we take it one step at a time? We'll figure that out when we get there."

Summer nodded. She loosened her grip on her phone, unaware until that moment that she'd been grasping it tight in anticipation of whatever he might say.

"You still there, Summer?"

"Yes, sorry," she whispered.

"Don't you go worrying about a thing, okay?"

"Okay."

His next words surprised her. "If the day comes when we both know you're not coming back, it'll all be all right. I promise you that."

She felt tears well up in her eyes, though she didn't understand why. "Thanks, Clay."

"Yeah. I have to go. Safe travels, little girl." He hung up.

She'd guess from his gruff tone, that he felt a little emotional, too, and again, she didn't understand why.

Chapter Two

Carter leaned his shovel against a tree and wiped his sleeve across his brow. The days were definitely getting warmer, but not warm enough to warrant the sweat he'd worked up this morning. That was all down to working his ass off. He was going at it hard in an attempt to keep his mind busy. He was back in Cassidy's yard, digging holes for a second line of aspens, since she'd loved the first so much.

He walked over to his truck to get a bottle of water. While he took a drink, he admired the view. Despite having lived in the valley his whole life, he still appreciated its beauty. On days like today, with a clear blue sky and the green returning after the long winter, it was breathtaking. Cassidy's house was in a great spot where the river ran through the property—still rushing and swollen with the runoff from the spring melt. As he looked around, his mind returned to Summer, yet again. He'd walked down here with her a few times, taking the little path that followed the river from Beau's rental house where she'd been staying. Damn! Beau's rental house where she'd be staying again by tonight. And he still hadn't been over there! He checked his watch. He knew Beau would have had his housekeeping crew out there before Summer's return, but he needed to get over there himself and get the yard taken care of. He should go now, get it done before she arrived.

He put the lid on his water bottle and climbed into his truck. Just as he was heading back up the driveway, his phone rang. He pulled over to take the call.

"This is Carter."

"Carter, it's Cassidy."

"Is everything all right?" Why was that always his first response, he wondered.

"Actually, it isn't. I'm stuck down in Gardiner. I've got a flat tire."

"No problem. I'll come get you. I can be there in half an hour."

"Thanks, but I'll be fine. It's Summer I need you to get. She should be arriving in just over an hour and there's no way I'll be able to get there in time. Would you go?"

Carter closed his eyes and drew in a deep breath. So much for his resolve to stay the hell out of her way. He couldn't leave her stranded at the airport.

"Carter?"

"Sure."

"Thank you! She'll be arriving at the General Aviation building. Do you know it?"

"Yeah."

"Okay. Thanks. I'll let you go. You'll be cutting it fine to get there in time yourself."

"Do you want me to bring her to your house?"

"See what she wants to do. I'm guessing she'll probably want to get to her place and get settled back in. Have her call me, would you?"

"Will do. See you later."

"Thanks, Carter. Bye."

He hung up and shook his head. Cassidy was right; he would be cutting it fine to get to the airport in an hour. Here he was all sweaty and dirty, wearing worn-out work jeans and a faded plaid shirt, with no time to go shower and change. He turned the truck onto East River Road and headed up toward town. What did it matter anyway? This was who he was. There'd be no point primping and preening himself for Summer, even if he did have the time. He had to stop thinking like that. She was the big country music star. He was the yard guy! He'd do his good deed, go give her a ride from the airport, and then he'd have to put her out of his mind.

Just under an hour later, he pulled into the parking lot at the airport. He cut the ignition and sat there for a moment. He couldn't help smiling. He was about to see her again! And, despite all the ways he'd tried to tell himself it was a bad idea all the way here, he couldn't wait! He felt a little foolish as he pulled down the sun visor and checked himself in the mirror. He was glad he had as he wiped a smear of dirt off his cheek.

He got out of the truck and patted himself down with a wry smile. She'd seen him in his work gear before, and from the way she'd ogled at him then, she didn't seem to mind the look too much at all. He strode across the parking lot. Like it or not, here he came!

~ ~ ~

Summer looked around as soon as they came in through the door from the ramp. She'd been a little put out that the charter company had sent the same two pilots who had flown her before. They were nice enough guys, but one of them, Carl, was still hoping for a date. She'd been quite taken with him at first—until she met Carter. At least his copilot Justin, had taken the hint that Cassidy wasn't interested in him.

She was surprised not to see Cassidy there waiting. She scanned the lounge again, perhaps she was a few minutes late?

Carl put a hand on her shoulder. "It doesn't look like she's here yet. Don't worry, I'll wait with you."

Summer really didn't want him to, but it would be rude to refuse. "Thank you."

He grinned down at her and gestured toward one of the large sofas. "Shall we? Justin will be out with your bags in a minute."

She nodded and looked around again. Come on, Cassidy! Where was she? There was still no sign of her.

Carl looked out back through the doors to the ramp where Justin was waving at them. He was swiping his pass, but the door wouldn't open. Carl rolled his eyes at Summer. "I'd better go let him in."

Summer watched him go then turned back to look at the main doors to the parking lot. Her breath caught in her chest as they slid open, and in walked Carter! She felt a huge smile spread across her face. He was gorgeous! Absolutely gorgeous! He looked as though he'd come straight from work. His muscular legs were clad in worn, faded denims, with well-worn cowboy boots sticking out the bottom. A faded plaid shirt did its best to stretch across his muscular torso. He was a big guy—a big, muscly, gorgeous guy. Just the kind of guy who made her go weak at the knees. She was grateful she was already seated when he caught sight of her and smiled. Her weak knees couldn't stop her from leaping to her feet and running to him, though. When she reached him, she flung her arms around him and hugged him tight. She closed her eyes as his huge arms wrapped around her and held her to his chest. Neither of them spoke; they just held on tight. It felt so right, so good, she didn't want to break the moment. She wanted it to last forever!

Eventually she looked up at him. "I missed you."

Her heart filled up at the smile on his face. "I missed you, too."

"Summer! Are you okay?" Summer frowned and Carter let go of her and stood back as Carl came to join them with her bags. He gave her an inquiring look and then eyed Carter warily. "Is everything okay here?"

"Everything is just great thank you." She smiled up at Carter. "My friend came to get me."

Carter nodded.

"*This* is your friend? I thought Cassidy was coming?" asked Carl.

Summer wanted to tell him it was none of his business, and that he needed to stop looking at Carter like he was some kind of thug! "It is." She didn't even want to introduce them, she just wanted to get out of here.

As he had done so often in the short time she'd known him, Carter picked up on exactly what she wanted. He met Carl's gaze and nodded. "I'll take her bags from here."

As Carter reached to take the handles, Summer wanted to laugh as Carl held tight to them.

"I should bring them out to the car."

Carter shook his head and stared him down. "I said, I'll take them."

Summer had to hide a smile at the panic in Carl's eyes when Carter took a step toward him. He surrendered the bags quickly and backed off. Summer knew Carter would never harm a fly, but with his build and quiet, but determined manner, he must seem quite threatening to another guy. She almost felt sorry for Carl.

"Thanks again," she said with a smile. "We need to get going." Carter nodded and fell in step beside her as she turned and walked away.

"Bye," Carl called after them.

When they reached the doors she turned back to see him still standing there staring after her. She gave him a little wave. Poor guy. He'd never had a chance anyway.

Carter had stopped beside her. She smiled up at him. "Thank you so much for coming to get me! Is everything okay with Cassidy?"

He nodded. "She got a flat tire and asked me to come instead."

"Oh." Summer felt a little deflated herself at that. She'd been stupid to hope he might have *asked* if he could be the one to come to get her.

His brows came down and he gave her a puzzled look before starting out again toward his truck. "She wants you to call her. I'm sure you'll see her soon enough."

When they reached the truck, she put a hand on his arm. "What's the matter?"

He threw her bags in the back seat before he replied. "Nothing." He didn't meet her gaze.

"Carter, please. I'm so happy you came to meet me. I didn't know how it would be between us. I was afraid you wouldn't even want to talk to me. Please, don't shut me out."

He remained quiet for a long moment, still looking away from her.

"Look at me. Tell me what I did? For a moment there, I thought you were happy to see me. Now I'm starting to think I was wrong."

He finally met her gaze. His big brown eyes were sad. "You didn't do anything wrong. I'm sorry. You're right. I *didn't* want to talk to you. My plan was to stay the hell away from you. Then Cassidy couldn't come get you, and she asked me to. When you came running to me like that, hell, you made me the happiest guy on earth. But then you sounded disappointed that Cassidy hadn't come for you herself. And I remembered. I shouldn't be so happy to see you. Should I?"

She smiled. "I don't see why not. I'm just as happy to see you. And you got it wrong. I wasn't disappointed that Cassidy didn't come. I was disappointed that you hadn't come voluntarily. You came as a favor to her. Not because you wanted to."

He cocked his head to one side. "Don't you go thinking I didn't want to."

She raised an eyebrow at him. "You just said yourself, you'd planned to stay the hell away from me." Her voice cracked on the last couple of words. She was talking too much, but this was too important not to.

He put his hands on her shoulders and looked down into her eyes. "I did. But not because I want to."

She stared back into those big brown eyes. She couldn't believe they were being so honest with each other. But she was glad of it. She wanted to be sure he really did mean what she thought he did. "Why then?" she whispered.

He shook his head slowly. "I planned to stay away from you, because what I want more than anything in the world is to be around you."

She continued to look deep into his eyes.

He straightened up. "There, see. This is exactly why I should stay away. Leave it to big old dumbass me to embarrass us both. Come on, get in the truck and let's get you home." He walked around to the passenger door and held it open for her. She trotted after him and climbed in. "You are *not* a dumbass, Carter!"

He shook his head and closed the door before walking around to get in the driver's seat. "I think you've done enough talking for now. Your voice is tired; I can hear it."

She scowled at him as he started the engine and pulled out. He was right about her voice, but this wasn't a conversation she wanted to break off now they'd started it. "But..."

He held up a hand as he pulled up at the pay station to exit the parking lot. "But nothing. You're here to rest your voice, not to strain it more."

She nodded. Her throat was feeling terrible. She knew she'd overdone it.

She put a hand on his arm before he pulled away. "Promise me we can talk about this later."

He shook his head. "There's no point."

She raised her voice as much as she could, which was barely above a whisper. "Promise me. Or I keep talking now."

He turned to her. "You're a stubborn one, aren't you?" He was scowling, but there was the hint of a smile in his eyes.

She nodded. "Only when it's important."

He *did* smile at *that*. "Okay. We'll talk about it when we get you home, if you promise not to talk on the way." His smile faded. "We both know what I need to say though."

She opened her mouth to ask him what he meant, even though he was right and she already knew.

"No." He didn't give her chance to speak again. "No more talking."

She nodded. It could wait. She had the feeling she'd have a lot to say when they got to the house. No way was she going to let him stick with his plan of staying away from her.

~ ~ ~

Carter kept his eyes fixed on the road ahead. What had he been thinking? Why in hell had he told her how she'd made him feel when she came running to him like that? Why had he told her that he wanted to be around her more than anything else in the world? Because it was true! That was the simple answer. But it wasn't a good enough answer. He should have kept his big mouth shut! He joined the interstate and headed east. He stole a glance over at her; she was staring out the window, lost in her own thoughts. He had to wonder what they might be. Shit! She was supposed to call Cassidy—but he'd made her promise not to talk.

"Maybe you should text Cassidy," he suggested.

She smiled at him and nodded. Good, she was keeping her word. She fished around in her purse, looking for her phone. That made him smile. He had to wonder what she kept in there, it was such a huge purse for such a little lady. She rolled her eyes at him as she finally found the phone and brought it out. She knew what he was smiling at; he'd teased her about it before.

He returned his attention to the road while she tapped out a text, then kept on tapping—apparently deep in conversation with Cassidy. He'd never gotten the hang of texting as a means of real communication. It came in handy for a quick message now and then, but he didn't get how people could chat away on there. He also didn't get why people seemed to think he should reply instantly. If it was *that* important, why didn't they just call? As if on cue, his own phone rang. He didn't like to talk on it when he was driving and it seemed rude while

Summer was sitting there. He let it ring. Once it had finished, the voicemail tone sounded. Then it started to ring again.

Summer looked over at him. She was right. He should probably get it. Maybe it was something important.

"This is Carter."

"I know," said Shane with a laugh. "I wasn't expecting anyone else to answer."

Carter laughed. "Okay, smartass. What do you want?"

"To ask you to come to dinner."

"I already told you I can't do that."

"Yes, you can. I know she's in the truck with you, but Summer just told Cassidy that *she* can't come to dinner."

Carter shot a glance over at her. She was still tapping merrily away. "Why?"

"Because Cassidy told her you weren't coming, and apparently she won't come if you're not."

He shot another look at Summer. She smiled sweetly at him, giving him the feeling she knew who he was talking to. "I don't want to," he told Shane.

Shane laughed. "Yes, you do. And besides, you think if you don't come you'll be able to avoid whatever it is she wants to talk to you about, but you're wrong. If you don't come, she's just going to keep you at her place and make you talk to her anyway. You may as well admit defeat and say you'll come."

Carter thought about it. By the sounds of it, going to dinner at Cassidy's house would be easier than spending the time alone with Summer at her house. He blew out a sigh. "Okay."

"Great! We'll see you later." Shane hung up.

Summer looked over at him.

He pursed his lips. "You win."

Her smile said she knew exactly what he meant.

Chapter Three

When Carter turned into the driveway, Summer smiled at the sight of the house. She really did love the place. She'd only stayed here for a short time, but it had felt like a sanctuary. A safe place to hide and to rest. It was so beautiful, sitting as it did on the bank of the Yellowstone, with glorious views of the mountains all around.

Carter brought the truck to a stop outside the front door then looked over at her. "What time did you tell Cassidy we'd be over for dinner?" he asked.

"Seven."

He nodded and looked at the clock on the dash. "In that case, I'll bring your bags in for you and leave you to get settled. I need to head home to shower and change."

She hadn't been expecting that. He'd agreed that they could talk when he got her here. "But..." she croaked.

He shook his head with a finality she recognized. "But nothing. You need to rest your voice for more than just an hour. I need to get cleaned up and changed. There's nothing to argue about."

She nodded. She knew he was right. But she wasn't giving up, either. She climbed out of the truck and followed him up the steps. Once she'd unlocked the front door, he brought her bags inside.

"Where do you want them?"

She pointed down the hallway to her bedroom. Carter stopped in the doorway, looking uncomfortable.

Summer couldn't help smiling. He'd been over here a few times during her last visit, but she knew he was uncomfortable *invading her private space* as he'd put it. He'd made a big effort to stay out on the deck whenever he came, only venturing in as far as the living room when she insisted. She gestured toward the bed, knowing that would make him more uncomfortable still. As he placed her bags on it, she sat down and smiled up at him. "Thank you."

He nodded and backed away. He didn't stop until he reached the door. When he did he blocked the light.

She wished he'd come back, come sit beside her, talk to her, be honest with her about how he felt, let her be honest about how she felt. "Do you have to go right now?" she asked.

He'd taken his hat off and was twisting it in his hands as he stood there. He held her gaze for a long moment before he nodded. "I do. Get some rest. I'll come pick you up around six thirty." He turned on his heel and left.

She was tempted to run after him, but she knew there was no point. He'd be back in a couple of hours, and hopefully, by then she'd be able to talk for a little while—rather than croak or whisper, which seemed to be all she was capable of right now. She heard the front door close and a few moments later his truck pulled away. She lay back on the bed and stared up at the ceiling. What was she going to do? What could she do? She had no idea. She knew she wanted to do something. Carter was her ideal man—both physically and in personality. She'd

told Cassidy that it seemed as though someone upstairs had
listened to everything she wanted in a man and had put Carter
together, especially for her. He was kind, he was sweet, he was
caring. He knew who he was, he loved his life, and he loved
his work. She sighed. And his life and his work were right here
in Paradise Valley. How could they get involved with each
other when she would probably be leaving in three months'
time—and he would never leave! At the same time, wouldn't it
be crazy not to explore what they both obviously felt for each
other? How would they be able to avoid it? Unless they
avoided each other, which seemed to be Carter's solution. She
shook her head. She wasn't going to let him get away with that.
She wanted to spend time with him, even if it was only as
friends.

She got up from the bed and went through to the bathroom.
She couldn't kid herself that just friends would be enough. She
started the water running. She wanted to sit in the tub and
stare out the window at the mountain while she mulled it all
through.

~ ~ ~

When Carter got home, he let himself in through the back
door. He kicked his boots off and hung his hat in the
mudroom. He picked up the coffee mug he'd left on the
kitchen table this morning and rinsed it out. What a difference
a day made! This morning, he'd known that Summer was
coming back and he was determined to stick to his plan to
avoid her. Now here he was, not twelve hours later, and he'd
already picked her up from the airport, told her she'd made
him feel like the happiest guy on earth, and if that wasn't
enough, he was going back to see her later and taking her to
dinner with his brother and Cassidy!

He tidied the kitchen. He loved this house. He'd built it the third year the nursery did well. The nursery covered five acres, and when the five next door had come up for sale, he'd bought the lot and built his home next to his business. It wasn't anything grand, but it was nice. It was his. He went out back and stopped to pet a cat who came curling around his legs. "Hey, Buster," he said as he scratched behind his ears. "How you doing? Are you keeping the mice down for me?" Buster purred loudly in reply and rubbed his head against Carter's leg.

Carter smiled. "Yeah, right. I'll fill up you guys' food." He left food out for a whole bunch of cats who hung around out here. He claimed that they kept the mice down, but in reality he was just a soft ass and didn't like to admit it. He was so soft, in fact, that he'd turned one of sheds into a home for the cats. Buster had been the first stray to show up around here a couple of years ago. Carter had invited him to come stay in the house, but he didn't like to be cooped up. Carter had taken to leaving food and warm blankets out in the shed—the shed that had a broken board where a cat could squeeze in if they really wanted to. Buster had made the place his home, and then he started inviting his friends over. Nowadays there were at least a half dozen of them who hung out on any given night.

Once he'd filled up their food and made sure they had fresh water, he let himself back into the house. It was time to take a shower and figure out what he was going to wear tonight. He chuckled to himself—what was he, a girl? But it was important to him. He wanted to look good. He opened his closet and stared in there. It shouldn't be important, but it was. He'd already proved to himself that he wasn't going to be able to stay away from Summer. He'd already been more honest than he should have with her about how he felt. And she hadn't been horrified. He knew she liked him. He was starting to wonder whether he should just keep being honest—with himself as well as with her. He'd spent ten years of his life avoiding women, trying to save himself from more pain. Maybe Summer was the one who would help him get past that? He knew that life didn't happen without pain, but if you were going to take the risk, the potential reward had to be worthwhile. He couldn't think of any greater potential reward than Summer. If he wasn't prepared to take a risk on her, then he may as well hang up his boots right now.

He closed the closet door again. He'd figure it out after his shower. For now he headed for the bathroom and set the water running. He needed to get cleaned up and hopefully wash some of his fear and confusion away.

He pulled up back at her house at six thirty on the dot. She must have been watching for him; the front door opened as he climbed out of his truck. He smiled. She was so damned beautiful! She was small and fragile looking, but there was a strength about her, too. A strength he admired. She was dressed casual tonight in black jeans and a long white sweater. Her long blonde hair fell loose around her shoulders. She took his breath away. She waved and he started toward her, realizing that he'd been standing there staring like an idiot.

"How are you feeling?" he asked when he reached the door.

She nodded. "Better." She smiled up at him. "And you'll be relieved to hear that I think we should get going."

He raised an eyebrow. He wasn't relieved; if anything, he was a little disappointed. He'd been looking forward to a few minutes alone with her, before they went to Cassidy's place.

She laughed. "I'm not letting you off the hook. I still want us to talk, but I have to be realistic about how long my voice will last. I want to get to Cassidy's, have dinner, and then get you back here."

He shook his head with a smile. "We won't be able to get away from their place early, and knowing you and Cassidy, your voice will be all used up in the first half hour anyway. I think I'm safe for tonight."

She surprised the hell out of him when she stepped toward him, put her hands on his shoulders and stood on tiptoe to kiss his cheek. "Don't you believe it, Carter. You'll never be safe from me!"

He sucked in a deep breath as she stood back with a smile. It took everything he had not to close his arms around her and pull her against him. Maybe he needed to go back to his plan of avoiding her, because letting her get as close as she just had would only end up leading them to one place. The way the blood was rushing through his veins, pounding in his temples, he wanted to forget about their evening out and take her to that one place right now!

She misread his reaction and looked concerned. "Was that too much?"

He shook his head.

"What then?"

"It wasn't enough." Damn! He shouldn't have said it. But he'd had no choice. It was the truth.

Her eyes widened and two little spots of pink appeared on her cheeks. Then a smile slowly spread across her face. "I agree."

Oh, shit! What was he supposed to do with that? What he supposed to say even? "Come on, we'd better get going." He turned around and headed back to the truck. It was the only safe thing to do.

~ ~ ~

When they arrived at Cassidy's, Shane flung the door open and greeted them with a grin. "Welcome back, Summer! Come on in. The little lady is in the kitchen; I've got her chained to the stove."

Summer laughed and reached up to hug him as he held his arms out to her. She liked Shane. He was the perfect guy for Cassidy. "It's good to see you again, Shane."

"Come on through," called Cassidy. "And if you can manage to lock that asshole out on the porch when you come in, that'd be great."

Shane grinned at Summer and Carter. "She loves me really."

Carter laughed. "I don't know how she puts up with you."

Shane feigned a hurt look and put an arm around Summer's shoulders as he walked her through to the kitchen. "I'm glad you're back. You're the only one who's ever nice to me. These guys are mean!"

Summer smiled at Cassidy who was, indeed, at the stove. She smiled back as she waved a wooden spoon at Shane with a grin. "She does, but if you don't get out of this kitchen and out of my way…"

Shane let go of Summer and held up both hands. "Consider me gone!" He looked at Carter. "Come on, bro. The kitchen's no place for guys to be hanging out anyways. Come on out on the deck with me. We can leave the little women to it."

Summer laughed as the wooden spoon flew through the air, just missing Shane's ear. "Get out while you still can!"

"Yes, dear. Love you, dear," called Shane as the door closed behind them.

"I see you're settling in to nearly-wedded bliss, then," Summer said when the guys had gone.

Cassidy laughed. "We are. It's wonderful. I love that asshole to pieces!"

"I can tell. Oh, and let me see the ring! Typical that you went and got engaged as soon as I left."

Cassidy wiped her hands and came around the island to show Summer her engagement ring.

"Oh, Cass! It's beautiful. Congratulations!"

The smile on Cassidy's face said it all. She was happier than Summer had ever seen her. It was obvious that she'd found her match in Shane. She gave Summer a hug. "Thank you! And what about you? How have you been?" She shot a look toward the door. "How's Carter?"

Summer couldn't help smiling. "Carter is wonderful! You know I adore him."

Cassidy nodded. "So, my flat tire came at a good time?"

Summer had wondered about the timing. "Did you really have one?"

Cassidy shrugged. "Might have. Might not. All that matters is that you got a ride home."

"Thank you."

"I need more than that! How did it go? What's he said? What's going to happen with you two?"

"If only I knew what's going to happen. I have no idea. It was so wonderful to see him at the airport. But he told me he was planning to avoid me while I'm here. I understand why—and it might be the wisest thing to do. But, Cass, I don't want him to. I want to spend time with him. I want him to be my friend."

Cassidy snorted. "You were doing well, but don't start lying to me. You do *not* want him to be your friend. You want a whole lot more than that. And so does he. I can tell."

Summer nodded. "You're right. As always. But what do we do about it? Neither of us do casual, and casual is all it could be. His life is here. My life is in Nashville."

Cassidy gave her a stern look. "And have you given any thought to your life in Nashville? To your career? Last time we talked about it, you weren't even sure you wanted to keep singing—even if you could."

Summer heaved a big sigh. "Honestly. I haven't wanted to think about it. I feel as though I'd be jinxing myself."

Cassidy raised an eyebrow.

She shrugged. "I daren't let my mind go near the thought of stopping singing, because…well, I know it sounds silly, but…it feels as though I'm being ungrateful. Singing has been the best thing that's happened to me. If I think about giving it up, it might be taken away from me."

"Taken away from you?"

"I might not get my voice back. I might not be *able* to sing again. Like I said, I know it's silly. In fact it's probably just an excuse not to make any decisions until I have to."

Cassidy nodded. "That sounds more like it."

"Yeah, well I'm not Miss Head-on Full-on like you are. I don't want to face it until I have to."

"So what's your plan? Take three months here, see what the doctors say and then decide?"

"Yeah, that's about it."

"And what happens to Autumn in the meantime? And Carter, for that matter?"

Summer shrugged. That was the problem. She didn't want to make any decisions about her career until she had to, but there were other decisions that she *did* want to make. Decisions that would depend on what happened with her career. "I don't know, Cass! I don't want to hurt either of them. I don't want to screw either of them over, but how can I know anything, until I know whether I can sing again?" She could hear the croak in her voice as she finished—so much for not overdoing it!

Cassidy put a hand on her shoulder. "You need to decide what you want, not wait to see what's possible."

Summer nodded. She could only expect that from Cassidy, that's what she herself would do—take life by the horns and wrestle with it till it submitted to her will. Summer was more used to going along with whatever life dictated and making the most of it. It wasn't that she wasn't strong. It was just that life had always dealt her a pretty decent hand and she made the most of the opportunities presented to her. She'd never been in this kind of situation before—where she needed to figure out what she wanted and go after it, for the sake of the people she cared about as much as her own.

"Do you know what you want?"

She shrugged. She thought she did, but everything she wanted conflicted with something else she wanted! Deep down, she already knew she wanted to quit her career. But she didn't want to leave Autumn in the lurch—her sister's career was dependent upon her own. She didn't want to let Clay down either. He'd been so good to her and he had such faith in her. Much as she didn't want to let them down, she *did* want to see what might happen between her and Carter. And the only way to do that would be to decide that she was going to stay right

here. How could she get involved with him if she knew she
might have to break things off and go back to Nashville? He'd
loved and lost before and it had broken his heart. She had no
intention of being the woman who put him through that a
second time.

Cassidy patted her shoulder. "Take a little time. You'll work it
out. I'll help if you want me. Just..." She looked toward the
door at the sound of the guys laughing out on the deck.
"Don't take too long. I'd hate to see Carter get hurt."

Summer nodded sadly. So would she.

"I'd hate to see *you* get hurt, too. And I think the longer you
put off making your decision, the more likely that is. Be brave.
Be honest with Carter; be honest with Autumn. You'll work it
out. But for now, put a smile back on your face and give me a
hand."

"Okay." Summer was happy to make herself useful rather than
carry on with this conversation which was making her so
uncomfortable. Cassidy had made her realize that she had to
make some decisions sooner rather than later. She was going
to have to *direct* the flow of her life instead of just waiting
around to go with it.

Chapter Four

Carter watched Summer as she chatted with Cassidy. Dinner had been wonderful. Cassidy was a great cook, although she had claimed Summer was much better. Now they were all sitting out on the deck over the river enjoying a glass of wine. He didn't normally like to drink at all when he was driving, but he figured one glass was fine. Cassidy was asking Summer about her sister and Carter felt like he was prying, just listening to them. He knew Summer thought the world of her sister. He also knew that Autumn was a much tougher nut than Summer. Well, he didn't actually know that. He just assumed it. She was Summer's business manager, and he had read a couple of articles that mentioned her as a shrewd businesswoman.

Right now Summer was telling Cassidy about all the juggling Autumn had done to clear the schedule while she rested her voice, and to make sure none of her plans were canceled, they were simply postponed. It brought it home to him again that her life and her career were awaiting her return. The roller coaster he'd been riding since he learned she was coming back plummeted down again. What had he been thinking earlier, about risk and potential reward? There was no potential for reward if he got involved with Summer. He'd be setting a sure course toward heartbreak. She'd leave once she had her voice back and he'd be left behind.

"Have you heard anything from Beau lately?" Shane's question interrupted his train of thought.

He nodded. "I talked to him a couple of days ago. Just about business, though."

"Has he said anything about Dad's plans with the ranch?"

Carter shook his head. All the brothers were waiting for their father's announcement about how he wanted to divide up the ranch between them. Carter was fine with whatever happened. So were Shane and Mason, but Beau wasn't happy about it at all. They knew that their dad wanted to divide the ranch five ways; between the four of them and Chance. Beau was dead set against Chance being included, even though he'd been like a fifth brother for many years now. "Like I said, we only talked about the rental houses and he wants me to work on one of the properties he's putting up for sale. He knows I play dumb when he starts talking about Chance. Why do you ask?"

Shane sighed. "I ran into him in town the other day. He was ranting about it as usual. It seems he's not happy about much of anything at the moment. He's pissed that Mom and Dad are giving the big house to Mason and Gina. He's pissed that they've already told Chance that the cabin is his." He shrugged. "I don't know. I guess, since you explained to me why he is the way he is, I worry about him."

Carter had to smile at that. "How about that? The littlest brother is finally discovering that thing they call empathy."

Cassidy laughed. "I think that might be pushing it a bit, Carter. Let's just say he's realizing that people have their own pain and motivations. I think he's fascinated by them, purely because they don't revolve around him, and he always thought the whole world did."

Shane gave her a hurt look. "Here I am, trying to become a better man, to be worthy of the love of a good woman, and all you can do is make fun of me." He looked at Summer. "Told you these guys were mean."

Cassidy laughed. "I wasn't making fun of you. That was high praise. I'm very proud of the way you're coming to realize that you aren't the center of the universe after all!"

Shane rolled his eyes. "Back to the point. I've been thinking that he might just need to find himself a good woman and settle down. That might be just what he needs to make him get his head out of his ass. I mean it's worked for the rest of us, hasn't it?"

Carter stared at him. What did he mean by *the rest of us?* It had worked for Shane and for Mason. Carter just hoped Shane wasn't including *him*. He had found a good woman. Summer was amazing, but he didn't stand a snowball's chance in hell of settling down with her—and everyone at the table knew it.

Cassidy seemed to understand what he was thinking, as she so often did. She shot him a sympathetic look before turning to Shane. "Never you mind trying to straighten Beau out. You've found the best woman there is and you still haven't got your head all the way out of your ass. Work on yourself before you go meddling in anyone else's business."

Shane really was getting better about picking up on what other people were feeling. He gave Carter an apologetic look before making a face at Cassidy, then rolling his eyes at Summer again. "Just plain mean. Didn't I tell you?"

Summer laughed. "Poor Shane." She smiled at Carter before looking back at Shane. "I mean who knows, you could be right. Maybe finding the right person and settling down is what brings out the best in all of us."

Carter didn't dare hope that she might be talking to Shane about him.

~ ~ ~

It was dark by the time they got back to the house. It had been a great evening, and Carter had been right about not being able to get away early. Summer turned to him as he pulled up outside the front door. "I saved my voice, so don't go trying any excuses. You're coming in and we're going to talk."

She loved the slow smile that spread across his face. He nodded and came around to open her door for her.

Once they were inside she led him through to the kitchen. "Would you like a glass of wine?" she asked.

He shook his head. "No, thanks. I've had my one."

She was disappointed. She'd been envisioning the two of them sharing a glass of wine while they talked. She'd decided she was going to be completely honest with him—tell him how she felt and what her fears were. She was hoping he would do the same, and a glass of wine might help him open up a little.

He sensed her disappointment and relented. "All right. I'll have a small one."

Once they had their drinks, they went through to the living room. This was weird. He was her friend, they'd spent quite a bit of time together, but she was nervous. It felt like a first date. She was aware of the implications of every word and every move. She wanted them to talk, and she wanted to be able to look at him while they did. But she didn't want to sit in one of the big armchairs facing the sofa, in case he thought she was avoiding sitting beside him. She took the easy option and sat on the sofa, leaving Carter to decide whether to sit next to her, or opposite.

She was a little disappointed when he selected one of the armchairs and placed his glass on the side table. He looked as nervous as she felt.

"So, where do we start?" she asked.

He shrugged. "Part of me thinks we shouldn't start at all. Once we have this conversation, we can't take it back."

She let out a little laugh. "Maybe so, but we can't take it back anyway. Just because neither of us have *said* how we feel. We both know, don't we?"

He nodded, that slow smile spreading across his face. "We do. But..."

"But what?" her heart was hammering. She was afraid he was going to go back to his solution of avoiding her, and she didn't think she could stand that. It would drive her nuts to be here and not be able to see him.

"But what do we do about it?" He took a sip of his wine then set his glass back on the table before meeting her gaze. "We've said we're going to be honest with each other, so here goes. I like you, Summer. I like you a whole lot more than I should. I'd like to be more than your friend."

She nodded. Her heart was hammering even harder now. It made her so happy to hear him say the words out loud. "Me too."

His eyes widened.

"Why do you look surprised? Surely you already knew that?"

He nodded. "I guess I did, but it's still a shock to have you confirm it. A good shock. But, Summer, I'm a coward. You know my story with Trisha. I've avoided women for years, because I never want to feel that kind of pain again." He shook his head. "But you. You make me feel like it'd be worth it."

"Worth it?" She didn't understand.

"The pain is inevitable. You're going to leave. I'm going to get my heart broken. But you make me feel as though whatever time we get to spend together will be worth a lifetime of hurt afterward."

She sucked in a deep breath. "But I don't want to hurt you, Carter."

He smiled. "I know. That's part of who you are, part of why I like you so much. You'd never hurt a soul if there was any way you could help it. But the fact is, I'm going to hurt any which way this goes down. I could hide from you for the next three months. But every day would be torture, knowing you're here and I could be spending time with you. Or we could spend the time together, and then I'll have to watch you leave."

Summer sighed. She saw another option, but she didn't want to say it before she knew if it was a realistic one. "I feel the same way. If you plan to avoid me while I'm here, that will hurt me so much. I'll understand. But it'll hurt anyway. But I'm scared. I'm scared that if we do spend time together…" She couldn't help it, she let her eyes wander over him, taking in his gorgeous face, his big, strong arms, his broad chest and muscular legs. "…if we do get to know each other properly, I'm scared about what will happen afterward."

He nodded. "I'll survive."

She shook her head. She'd known he would think that she was only worried about hurting him. "Maybe, but I'm not sure I will."

His chin jerked up. "What are you saying?"

"I don't know. I don't know what I'm saying. I think I'm getting too far ahead of myself." She took a long sip of her wine. She really was getting ahead of herself. Maybe this whole conversation was too far ahead of itself. They barely knew each other. Yes there was an undeniable attraction between them, but... She smiled. "I guess I'm saying that I'm starting to feel uncomfortable. I guess I'm saying that all we really need to do is decide if we're both brave enough to give this a shot, and if we are, well, I guess we'll just have to see where it goes?"

He nodded slowly.

She waited. Was he nodding his agreement with what she was saying, or was he nodding that yes, he was brave enough to give it a shot.

When he finally spoke, her heart felt as though it was exploding in her chest. "I'm brave enough if you are."

She grinned and raised her glass to him. "I certainly am. Here's to being brave."

He touched his glass against hers and then downed the whole thing.

She did the same.

His smile was different. He seemed more relaxed and she was pretty sure the wine hadn't affected him that rapidly.

He held her gaze for a long moment. "I guess I didn't realize how uptight I was feeling. It's funny, isn't it, the relief that comes with making a decision."

She nodded.

"Even if it might be a *really* bad one."

Oh, she didn't want him to feel that it was a bad decision! She got up and went to him, and did something she'd been longing to do since the first day she met him. She sat down in his lap and looped her arms up around his neck. "Let's make sure it's a good one," she said. It already felt like the best decision she'd ever made. His arms had automatically closed around her. It felt as though he surrounded her, and it felt so right. He was so big, so muscular, and hard. She shifted a little. His muscles weren't the only hard thing! He lowered his gaze and turned his head away. She didn't want him to feel embarrassed! She tucked her fingers under his chin and made him look at her. "I don't know why you're looking like that. I take it as a compliment."

The corners of his mouth turned up. "It's a compliment all right, darlin'. You have no idea what you're doing to me." A low deep chuckle rumbled up from his chest. "I could compliment you all night long."

Ooh! She liked the sound of that! She raised an eyebrow at him, but he shook his head. "You already know me better than that. I'm a good old-fashioned boy. There'll be no rushing with that."

She pouted, she couldn't help it. That chuckle rumbled up again. He brought his hand up to her cheek and sank his fingers into her hair. "You can sulk all you like, but it'll be worth the wait."

She stared into his eyes, her body reacting to his words. She couldn't wait! But she knew she'd have to. She brought her hands up to his shoulders and brought her face closer to his. Then she waited. And waited. "Are you going to kiss me, or not?"

His arms tightened around her as he pulled her against his chest. He held her gaze until his lips met hers. He ran his tongue along her bottom lip, making her sigh. Then his mouth claimed hers in a kiss that left her with no doubts that he'd be worth the wait. She'd never been kissed like that in her life. With one arm, he crushed her to his chest; his other hand tangled in her hair, pulling her head back to give him better access to her mouth. She clung to his shoulders as she kissed him back. When he eventually lifted his head, her breath was coming low and shallow. She wanted more—so much more. From the way he kept shifting under her, she knew he did too. No matter how much he tried to move away, the bulge in his pants was pressing into her, letting her know that that part of him, at least, had no more patience than she did. She squirmed in his lap, but he shook his head.

"I should go."

"No! I don't want you to, and I don't think you do either." He couldn't go now!

"That's exactly why I should go."

"But you just had all that wine!" She felt bad, but his safety on the road wasn't really her first concern.

It made him hesitate though. "I *have* to go." He sounded less adamant now.

"There's a spare room," she said with a smile. "I promise I'm not trying to keep you just so I can have my wicked way with you. I just don't want you to go yet."

He thought it over for a few moments. "Okay. I'll stay." She loved the way his eyes twinkled as he added, "But you have to promise; no funny business. No sneaking into my room in the middle of the night."

She laughed. "Okay. I promise. But you can sneak into mine if you like."

He chuckled. "No I can't, even though I would like. We're going to do this right."

She nodded. She wasn't used to a guy who wanted to take his time, but it was part of Carter's charm. He was a true gentleman. "Okay then." She reached for her glass, but it was empty. "Would you like another, since you don't have to worry about driving now?"

He nodded and followed her into the kitchen. When she turned back to hand him his glass, he looked troubled.

"What is it?"

"Nothing. Well, maybe something. I'm wondering how this is going to work. I mean, my first thought was that I want to take you out to dinner—on a date. But…well, can we do that? Do you want to be seen out with me? Is that a problem? What about your sister?"

Summer put a hand on his arm. "It's okay. Autumn's okay about it. She wasn't really mad because she thought I was seeing you. She was mad because…" How could she explain all of that? By being honest was the only way. "She was mad because she thought I'd given up on my singing. She thought I was afraid I'd never get my voice back, and that I'd gone out to find myself a man and a different kind of life by way of consolation."

"I see." Carter really didn't look as though he did see at all.

"Don't you go thinking that's what I am doing!" She'd hate him to think that.

He shook his head. "The thought hadn't crossed my mind."

"What then?"

"I was wondering how bad your voice is, if your sister sees that as a possibility."

Summer sighed. "I don't know. It's called a granuloma. It's like a little hard growth on my vocal chords. It's more common than you might think. It might go away without surgery—that's the hope—if I rest it enough."

Carter gave her a pointed look. He was right. She was talking way too much today.

She shrugged. "I know, but we could hardly have said everything we needed to if I had to write my side down could we?"

He shook his head. "And what if you do need surgery?"

She shrugged. "I don't know. I don't know if I'd want to. There's no guarantee the vocal chords wouldn't be damaged or that the stupid thing wouldn't grow back again afterward. It's just a game of wait and see right now. But, the point is, you don't need to worry about Autumn. She knows I like you and she knows I was hoping we might..." Oops, maybe that was saying too much.

He raised an eyebrow with a smile. "You were hoping we might what?"

She shrugged. "Get to be more than friends."

"We will. We are."

She nodded. "So how about we take our wine out on the deck and look at the stars?"

He surprised her by shaking his head. "No."

"Why not?"

"Because, it's cold out there. You don't seem to be doing a very good job of taking care of yourself, so I'll help. You don't need to be out in the cold air. You're talking plenty and you're not sounding too bad." He gave her a mock stern look. "But I think that might be the wine lubricating your throat."

She sighed. He was right, of course. "So what do you want to do instead?"

He made his way back to the living room and sat on the sofa, patting the space beside him with a grin. "I told you I'll take care of you. I want to do something that will stop you from talking for a while—and keep you warm, too."

Oh my! He was so damned sexy! She'd thought he didn't even know it, but the sparkle in his eyes right now said he knew damn well the effect he was having on her. She gladly sat down beside him and smiled up at him. "And what kind of something would that be?"

He closed his arms around her and drew her to him. "This," he said in the moment before his lips came down on hers.

Chapter Five

Carter opened his eyes and looked around. It took him a minute to remember. He was at Summer's place. He drew in a deep breath then slowly let it out. In her spare room. Was he crazy, or what? They'd made out on the sofa in the living room for hours last night. She'd tried everything she could think of to get him out of his pants—and into hers. He shifted uncomfortably as his body woke up at the memory. And he, big old dumbass that he was, he'd turned her down—repeatedly. What kind of guy lay on the sofa, making out with his dream girl and refused to take her to bed? What kind of guy turned down the opportunity to spend the night with Summer Breese? He shook his head. He did. He didn't just want to spend the night with her. He wanted to spend time with her. Of course he wanted to sleep with her, but he wanted more than that. He wanted to build something special with her, so that by the time they did go to bed it would mean something. He started at the sound of her moving around downstairs. He checked his watch. Damn! It was seven thirty already! He scrambled out of bed and pulled his jeans on. He grabbed his socks and shirt and headed downstairs.

When he reached the kitchen he stopped and stared. She had her back to him as she fixed the coffee. She was wearing a pink sleep shirt. It barely covered her ass and left her long, slender, tanned legs bare. He ran his gaze over them, all the way down to where her ankles disappeared inside a pair of pink, fluffy slipper boots. He'd always thought that women who tried to do 'cutesy' needed to grow up. He was revising his opinion rapidly as he watched her move about the kitchen. Cute was the new sexy in his mind.

It was only when she turned around that he realized he was standing there staring, socks and shirt in his hand. She smiled and let her eyes drop to his chest. He clutched his shirt tighter. Jesus! What was he thinking? She was looking at him as if she wanted to eat him up and he was trying to cover his modesty with his shirt? He let his hands fall by his sides as he smiled back at her.

"Good morning."

"It's a very good morning!" she replied.

He cocked his head to one side. "It is? Why's that?"

"Because it's my first morning back in Montana. I get to wake up in this beautiful place, and even better I get to start the day with a beautiful man standing half naked in my kitchen."

He smiled. "Sorry. I panicked when I saw the time." He started to put his shirt on.

She came over to him and placed both her hands on his chest. He had to close his eyes and take a deep breath, and he had to remind himself that he was the guy who didn't want to sleep with Summer Breese—yet! His body begged to differ. It didn't want to wait another second. Not with the way her hands felt as they stroked across his chest and up to his shoulders. Not with the way her breasts felt as they pushed at his chest when she stepped closer. Not with the way her fingers felt as they sank into his hair and pulled his head down for a kiss. He closed his arms around her and pulled her close, loving the feel of her pressed against him. He wanted nothing more in that moment than to lift her off her feet, carry her back upstairs, and make it a very good morning indeed. But he resisted. He kissed her softly then stepped back. He had to smile at the disappointment on her face as she looked up at him.

He shrugged. "I have to get to work."

"Oh."

That made him chuckle. "Don't sound so surprised."

"Sorry, I just don't want you to go."

"I don't *want* to, but I *have* to. And I think I'd better put my shirt on before I step outside, don't you?"

He loved the way her gaze lingered on his chest before he shrugged into his shirt. His brothers always teased him about his physique. He was proud of the body he'd built, but he'd done it for himself—not to draw admiring glances from women. The way Summer looked at him made him feel even more justified in spending so much time in the gym.

She smiled. "I suppose you'd better cover up, yes."

He nodded and buttoned his shirt, trying to hide his smile at the way she watched.

She looked up at him with a sheepish grin. "Sorry. I'm being a little brazen, aren't I? But you're so hard to resist. You're gorgeous and I can't hide the fact that I think so."

He chuckled. "Please don't apologize. I love it! I'm glad you like what you see." He allowed his own gaze to drop from her face and take in her pert little breasts, her gorgeous figure, and her slender legs. He smiled and bit his bottom lip. "I'm just trying to be more discreet about how much I like what I see."

She tucked her fingers under his chin and made him look her in the eye again. "Well, I'm glad you do like it. I'm freezing my ass off here, in the hopes you would like. But once you've gone I'm getting straight back into my warm, fleecy PJs."

He laughed, pleased that she'd made the effort to wear something sexy for him, and even more pleased that she was happy to admit it. "I'd offer to stick around and help you get warm, but that may not be the best idea."

"I think it's a great idea!"

He laughed again. "So do I, but I think it will be even better if we take our time and get there the right way." He looked into her eyes. "I want you, Summer. I can't lie. But you only get one first time. I want to make it right."

She nodded. "So do I."

All of a sudden he felt as though he'd said too much. He bent down to put his socks on and then hopped around to get into his boots. "I have to go. I'll call you later." He made for the front door, but stopped when he reached it. She'd followed him with a worried look on her face. He smiled. "I'm running out on my embarrassment, not on you."

Her face relaxed as she smiled back. "There's nothing to be embarrassed about, Carter."

"I know, and I'll be damned if that doesn't make me feel even more embarrassed. So let me make my undignified exit, huh?"

She gave a little laugh and put a hand on his shoulder. "Okay. As long as you promise you'll call me later."

He laughed at that. As if he could forget! "You have my word."

"Thank you." She stood on tiptoe and pecked his cheek.

It was all he could do to stop himself from pulling her to him. Instead he cupped her face between his hands and planted a gentle peck on her forehead. "See you."

~ ~ ~

Summer sighed as she watched his truck disappear. She shouldn't be disappointed that he had to go to work. He had a business to run, a life to live. But she *was* disappointed nevertheless. She shouldn't be disappointed that she hadn't been able to persuade him into her bed—last night or this morning. He was a gentleman and he wanted to take his time. But she was disappointed nevertheless. He was so damned sexy! He did funny things to her insides. She wanted him. She didn't want to wait! But part of her was glad that they hadn't gone to bed together. There was no need to rush. He was right; they should take their time. She went back to the kitchen and poured herself a cup of coffee. As she took it through to the living room, she couldn't help but think that they shouldn't take too much time. Not if they were only going to have three months together. She sat down in the big armchair beside the window where she could admire the view. They couldn't have anything more than that. Could they?

Sitting there sipping her coffee and staring out at the beautiful mountains, she had to wonder. Last night, talking with Cassidy, she'd realized that she would have to decide for herself what she wanted her future to hold. If that was the case, then she really ought to start thinking about what mattered most to her. She sighed. How could she do that just yet? Carter was a big part of why she was even considering staying here in the valley. And how could she make a decision based on him and her feelings for him? They hadn't even been out on a date yet. She smiled through pursed lips—hadn't even slept together yet. Surely she needed to take more time? Ugh. This was like a vicious circle. She needed to make up her mind because they had so little time. She couldn't make up her mind because they'd had so little time. What was a girl supposed to do? She shrugged and took her mug back through to the kitchen. This girl was going to do what she always did. She was going to take a shower, make herself presentable, and *then* figure it out!

An hour later she was showered, dressed, and had her makeup on. She looked like Summer Breese, the country music artist. Which meant she felt like shit! She wandered around the house. The beauty of this place was that she didn't *have* to do anything. She was here to rest, but today she didn't feel like resting. She wanted to do something. She was antsy. She should head up to town. She needed to shop for groceries, but she was a little nervous about going out in public by herself. The people of the valley had been great last time she was here and they'd left her in peace. Many of them had seemed to recognize her when she'd been up to town, but no one had made a fuss. Some had smiled and waved. Others had nodded in recognition, but no one had come up to her and harassed her. She'd been grateful for that. The article that had run in the local paper had her worried now. She knew it was just that Angie, and hoped it was a one-off.

She picked up her phone. She'd check with Cassidy first; she'd either set her at ease or tell her to stay home. There'd be no mincing of words from her old friend and she was grateful for that.

She dialed the number and waited.

"Hey, chica! What did you get up to last night?"

"What do you mean?" Summer was surprised that she was automatically on the defensive.

Cassidy laughed. "I didn't mean anything, but now you've got me curious. Carter hadn't showed up at my place before I left this morning. Did you keep him out late?"

Summer smiled to herself as she wondered what to say.

"Come on! Your silence speaks volumes!"

She laughed. "No. That's just *your* imagination talking!"

"So put me out of my misery! What happened?"

"Nothing. He stayed the night at my place."

Summer held the phone away from her ear as Cassidy squealed. "What? Make up your mind. Nothing happened or he stayed the night?"

"Both!"

"Let me get this straight. He stayed, but nothing happened?"

"Well, something happened."

"I knew it!"

"Not that! What happened was that we finally talked to each other about how we feel…"

"And?"

She had to laugh. "And I'm about to tell you if you give me chance!"

"Oh. Sorry. Go on."

"We decided that we're going to start seeing each other…"

"Yay!"

"Will you stop interrupting?"

"Shit. Yes. I'll have to. I've got customers. Can I call you back?"

"I'll tell you what, how about I come up to town. I can come into the gallery to see you. And if you have time we can go for lunch."

"Do you have a car yet?"

"Yes. The rental guys must have dropped it off while we were at your place last night."

"Great. Get your little ass on up here then. Drive safely. I'll see you soon."

"On my way."

Half an hour later, Summer could only manage to find a parking spot quite a way down Main Street from the gallery. She locked the car and started walking.

"Summer!"

She froze at the sound of her name being called by a man's voice she didn't think she recognized. She cautiously turned around, wishing she hadn't stopped at all. A rush of relief swept through her when she saw Beau Remington hurrying toward her.

"Sorry," he said when he reached her, "I shouldn't go around shouting your name like that, should I?"

She smiled. "That's okay."

He shook his head. "No, it isn't. I won't do it again. Where are you going anyway? Should you be out by yourself like this?"

"I'm going to the gallery to see Cassidy. This is as close as I could park."

"I'll walk with you, if you like. I'm heading that way."

"Thanks."

He fell in step beside her. "Is everything okay at the house?"

"It's great, thank you. I do love that place."

"Enough to buy it?"

She looked up at him. He was smiling, but it was a serious question.

"I don't know yet. Are you in a hurry to get it sold?"

He shook his head. "Not at all. Just curious if you're really interested."

"I might be. I just don't know yet."

"That's okay. You've got first refusal if you want it. I'm happy to rent it to you for as long as you like."

"Thanks, Beau. I appreciate it."

He nodded.

She wondered what else to say to him. She'd met all the Remington brothers and found the other three to be very easy company. She wasn't so sure about Beau, and she wondered if that was fair. Was she simply basing that on what she'd heard others say about him? He'd been nothing but pleasant to her. Well, he had been the one who'd brought Angie to Cassidy's house that night, but what Angie had done was hardly his fault.

They walked on in silence a little ways before he turned to her with a smile. Just like his brothers, he was a very handsome guy.

"Do you mind if I say something?"

She smiled back. "Well, I won't know until you say it, will I? So you'd probably best just go ahead."

He nodded. "I'm not one to interfere in other people's lives. That's not my intention here at all…"

As he searched for his next words, Summer thought she knew what was coming. She was right.

"Carter. I think you know his history?"

She nodded. "I do."

Beau looked uncomfortable. "I don't think you'd ever hurt him on purpose, but please be careful."

She nodded again. "I will. I am. I wouldn't't."

She stared up at him and they both started to laugh.

"So, you do know what I mean, then. I wasn't sure if I should say anything."

"It's okay. I'm glad you did. We're going to take it slowly and just see what happens."

Beau's expression told her he was surprised. It made her wonder whether she shouldn't have said anything at all, but it was too late now.

He nodded. "I'm glad. I was worried he might just go to ground and avoid you now you're back."

She smiled. "So was I."

They arrived in front of the gallery and stopped. "I guess I'll see you around," said Beau.

Summer nodded. She hoped so. She liked Beau. She wondered what Shane meant when he'd said he worried about him. "I'm thinking about having everyone over to dinner once I get settled back in. I hope you'll come?"

"Thank you." He looked so different when he smiled. "I'd like that. And don't worry. I'll come alone. I feel really bad about what Angie did."

"Please don't. It wasn't your fault. You couldn't have known."

He shrugged. "I shouldn't have brought her. I just didn't want to come by myself."

That surprised Summer. Beau seemed so confident, she wouldn't have thought he'd care about going to a dinner party alone, or what anyone would think of him not having a date. "Well, you bring someone if you want to, or you're more than welcome to come by yourself. Either way is fine. I just hope you'll come."

"Thanks. I will. And if there's anything you need—anything with the house—don't hesitate to call me."

"Thanks."

She turned at the sound of the gallery door opening. Cassidy poked her head out. "Why don't you both come on in?"

Beau shook his head. "I have to get going. I just didn't like Summer walking here by herself." He smiled at Cassidy, then at Summer. "I guess I'll see you around."

"I'll call you," said Summer.

"Yeah, see ya," said Cassidy.

Once he'd gone Summer followed Cassidy inside. "What was that about?"

"What was what?"

Cassidy grinned. "I thought you and Carter were just getting started. What's with you calling Beau?"

Summer laughed. "About having everyone over for dinner, silly!"

"You want to invite him again after what happened last time?"

"That wasn't his fault! He's a nice guy. I feel a bit sorry for him; it seems like he's the outcast of the family."

Cassidy frowned. "I wouldn't go that far. He's not exactly an outcast, he's just not as close as the other three are. But it strikes me that that's by his choice, not anyone else's."

Summer shrugged. "Maybe, but I don't think he's as bad as everyone makes him out to be."

Cassidy laughed. "There goes my little bleeding heart, Summer. You're too soft. Anyway, enough about Beau. It's Carter I want to hear about. What happened last night? Come on through to the back and you can tell me all about it."

Chapter Six

Carter looked up at the sound of a truck approaching. Mason. What was he doing here? He walked around the house to meet his brother as he pulled up.

"How's it going?" asked Mason as he got out of the truck.

Carter nodded. "It's going well. We're just getting finished up here. Should have everything finished by the end of the week. I'm sure Cassidy will be glad to have us out of her hair finally."

Mason looked around. "You've done a great job on the place."

Carter nodded. "I can't take much credit for this one. Old Mr. Allen had already drawn up what he wanted to do with the place before he sold it to Cassidy. She liked what he'd come up with and added a few touches of her own. I just did the grunt work."

Mason smiled and shook his head. "Nah, sorry, Carter. I'm not buying it. Mr. Allen drew up his plans under your guidance and Cassidy sought your advice on everything she wanted. You can say what you like, but I can tell, this place is one of your designs. It's got your name written all over it."

Carter dropped his gaze and toed the gravel.

"Don't be so modest." Mason grasped his shoulder. "Own your genius."

Carter had to laugh at that. "I'd hardly call it genius. I'm just good at knowing what to plant where. It's not exactly rocket science."

Mason gave his shoulder a gentle shake. "There are different kinds of smart, you know. I could never do what you do. Hell, I bet there aren't any rocket scientists who could."

Carter had to laugh at that. "Thanks, Mase. But I'm fine with who I am. You don't need to build me up every time we talk."

Mason let go of his shoulder and punched his arm. "Who says I'm trying to build you up? If you must know, I was trying to sweeten you up, since I have a favor to ask."

"Well, you don't need to sweeten me up for that. Of course I'll help. What do you need?"

Mason laughed. "Don't you think you should find out what I need *before* you say you'll help? You don't know what you're letting yourself in for. You might hate the idea."

Carter shrugged. "It doesn't matter. Whatever it is, I want to help." It was true. Helping his brother and taking care of his family was more important than any inconvenience it might cause to himself.

"I wondered if you could give me a hand this weekend. I've been training some horses for the McLellan Ranch. They said they didn't need them out there until the end of the month, but now they need them back next weekend. They're pretty much ready to go, but I want to put them through a final bombproofing this weekend. Make sure none of them have any spook left in 'em."

Carter nodded slowly. He'd helped Mason out with the horses many a time in the past. He enjoyed riding them through scenarios that might frighten them. Mason trained them to cross water, pass fire, pass waving flags, all kinds of things. He liked to bombproof them, as he called it, before the ranches trusted them to take visitors out on the trails. The only problem was Carter had been planning on spending as much time as he could with Summer this weekend.

Mason studied his face. "Problem?"

"No, no problem. When do you need me?"

Mason made a face. "For the weekend, if you can?"

Carter nodded again. "Okay."

Mason laughed. "You can say no, you know."

Carter shook his head. He couldn't. He didn't want to. He wouldn't let his brother down when he needed his help. "It's fine. I'll be there."

"Thanks." Mason looked puzzled. "Are you sure? Is everything okay?"

"Everything's just fine." Carter grinned at his brother. "But if you're done. I need to get back to work. I want to get this place finished up once and for all."

"Sure," said Mason. "I'll leave you to it."

Carter watched him drive away. He'd still be able to see Summer. Who said she'd want to spend the whole weekend with him anyway? He walked back around the house. He needed to get the last of the aspens planted, then put the final touches on the patio and his work here would be done. He might even get finished up early enough that he could hit the gym. He'd like to fit in a workout before he saw Summer tonight. He should call her. He didn't know if she wanted to go out to dinner, or if she'd rather keep a low profile. Part of him hoped she did want to go out. That'd make it easier to stick with his plan of taking it slow. He wasn't sure he could make it through another night of making out on the sofa with her without taking it further. He shook his head. He really needed to get to the gym and work off the frustration building up in his body!

Just as he got started back on the aspens, his phone rang in his back pocket. He pulled it out.

"Hey, Beau. Is everything all right?"

Beau laughed. "Yes, dammit! Have I ever called you because it's not?"

Carter shrugged. He needed to find another way to answer his phone, but he did worry. "Sorry. What is it?"

"Nothing. I mean. I just wanted to check in with you."

Carter frowned. That wasn't like Beau. He might not call because something was wrong, but he sure as hell never called just to shoot the shit either. "About what?"

"Okay. You got me. I ran into Summer in town."

"And?"

"And as much as you all think I'm an asshole, I care about you, okay? What are you thinking? What's happening with the two of you?"

Carter had to laugh. Mason was the one who, as the eldest, normally looked out for his brothers. Beau was generally oblivious to what was going on in the others' lives. Today it seemed the roles were reversed.

"What's so funny?"

"Nothing. It just tickles me to know you care. Thanks, Beau. Don't worry though. It's all good."

"I hope so."

"Why? What makes you think it wouldn't be?"

"Nothing. I like Summer. She seems like a decent person. It's just you. This is the first time I've seen you interested in anyone since Trisha, and it's not exactly a straightforward situation is it?"

Carter sighed. Beau was right, of course. It wasn't. "I know, but what can I do? It's just my luck that the only woman who's caught my eye happens to be a country music superstar who's only going to be in my life for three months before she leaves and breaks my heart!"

Beau was quiet for a long moment.

"Hey, come on. It is what it is. I'm not as stupid as I make out. I know the score. I was going to try to stay away from her, but that's really not an option. So, I'm choosing to make the most of the time that she's here. It's better to have loved and lost and all that, right?"

"Are you sure?" asked Beau. "I remember you saying you'd rather never have loved at all after Trisha."

Carter sighed. He remembered saying that, too. "I know. But that was different. I thought me and Trisha were forever. I was totally blindsided by what she did. It's not like that with Summer, is it?"

"I guess not. If the two of you don't work out it will be because of circumstances, because of life."

"Yep, and I'm old enough and wise enough to get that now. I'm making a choice, and part of that is understanding the consequences and accepting that I'll have to live with them."

Beau sighed. "Sounds as though you've got your head screwed on right."

Carter laughed. "Thanks, I think."

"I'm here for you, okay?"

Carter smiled to himself. That meant the world to him, especially coming from Beau. "Thanks."

"Yeah, okay, well I'm going." He laughed. "And don't you breathe a word of this conversation to anyone else, will you?

I've got my reputation as an asshole to think about. I wouldn't want you blowing that. See ya."

Carter chuckled himself as he hung up. Beau was no more an asshole than any of them. He was just a bit uptight about things that didn't matter to the others. His heart was in the right place and *that* was what really mattered.

He decided he may as well call Summer while he had his phone out. Hopefully then he'd be able to get finished with Cassidy's yard without any more interruptions. He dialed the number and waited while it rang.

"Hi, Carter."

He smiled at the sound of her voice and at the realization that she must have his number saved. "Hey." He kept on smiling to himself, then remembered that he might need to actually say something. "I said I'd call."

"I'm glad you did."

"Have you decided what you'd like to do later?"

"I was thinking I could make you dinner."

He took a deep breath. That would mean spending the evening at her house again. Did it also mean that she didn't want to be seen out with him?

"Is that okay?"

"Yeah, that's great. Do you want me to bring anything?"

"Just yourself."

He pursed his lips. He knew what she wanted to do with him, too! "What time?"

"As soon as you can get there."

"Okay. I'll call you when I'm leaving my place."

"Great. See you later."

"Bye." He hung up and wiped his sleeve over his eyes. He really needed to get to the gym! Maybe he could take her out for a walk down by the river. He'd have to do something. He closed his eyes and pictured her the way she'd been this morning in that cute, sexy night shirt. Damn! He wanted a fast forward button so he could hurry up and take his time!

~ ~ ~

Summer hung up and smiled to herself. She wasn't at all worried about going out in public with Carter. She just wanted him all to herself!

Cassidy gave her a knowing look. "Got your evening planned then, have you?"

She nodded. "I do. I'm going to cook for him."

Cassidy laughed. "Yeah, right. You just don't want to let him take any more time!"

"Well, there is that, too!"

"Poor guy. He's trying to do the decent thing and take it slow and you're planning on ravishing him!"

Summer laughed. "It's true! But I can't help it. I've wanted to ravish him since the first time I laid eyes on him. I mean, who wouldn't? He's gorgeous! He's so damned sexy."

Cassidy laughed. "Well, don't force him. It might do you good to take it slow."

Summer sighed and looked around. They were sitting in the back room of the gallery. Cassidy had gone for sandwiches from the coffee shop and brought them back here. She hadn't been so much worried about Summer going out in public as she was interested in being able to have a private conversation about Carter. "You're probably right. I keep thinking that myself. And he's so sweet. He even said you only get one first time and he wants it to be special. I do too, but I just don't want to wait!"

"Aww, he's a sweetheart," said Cassidy. "Don't rush him. Let him take his time and make it special."

Summer nodded. "I know. I should. But at the same time, I keep thinking if we're only going to have three months, I want us to make the most of every moment we can. Why wait?"

Cassidy gave her a long hard look. "Because the best things in life are worth waiting for, that's why."

Summer stuck her tongue out. "I bet you and Shane didn't wait."

Cassidy laughed. "As a matter of fact we did. I made him wait. I sent him home all horny and desperate."

"I find that hard to believe. How *long* did you make him wait?"

"Okay, so he was back at six o'clock the next morning. Still horny and…yeah."

Summer laughed. "Yeah. That's more like it."

"Still, though. Carter's different."

Summer smiled. Yes, he was—very different. Very special. "I know. I'll try to be good."

Cassidy looked up at the sound of the buzzer signaling someone had come into the gallery. "I'd better go see to them," she said.

Summer ate her sandwich while she waited. She couldn't help smiling to herself at the thought of her evening ahead. She should get going soon. She wanted to go to the grocery store to get stocked up and get everything she'd need for dinner. She loved to cook, and she was looking forward to cooking for Carter. She smiled as she wondered what she should make for dessert. Whipped cream would be good! No. She needed to stop thinking like that. She should let Carter go at his own pace.

Cassidy came back in.

"That was quick."

"Yeah, it was just one of the ladies from my seniors' art class. We've invited them to our engagement bash." Cassidy chuckled to herself. "They're a hoot and they did play a part in bringing me and Shane together."

Summer made a face. "So you've invited them, but not me?"

"Oh, shit! I didn't even think! We did all the planning last week. Of course you're invited. That goes without saying."

Summer laughed. "Don't worry. I was only teasing. I'm just surprised that I hadn't even heard mention of it. What are you doing? When is it?"

"A week from Saturday. We've booked one of the function rooms up at Chico."

"Great. I've never been there."

"You'll love it. It's really cool. It's like a little resort. There's the hot springs and a lodge and guest cabins and then the saloon, and the restaurant is fabulous. Get this! They call it the dining room!"

Summer smiled. "It sounds awesome. And the restaurant is good?"

Cassidy nodded. "The food's great and they have a wonderful wine cellar."

Summer nodded thoughtfully. "And it's open during the week?"

"Yeah, why?"

"Maybe Carter and I should go there tonight. Going out for dinner might make it easier for me to resist temptation. I think I'll be tempted to trip him up and beat him to the floor if we spend the whole evening at my place."

Cassidy laughed. "If you're that horny, then maybe the two of you *should* go out."

Summer nodded. Maybe they should. She jumped as the back door opened behind her.

"Hey, G," said Cassidy. "Look who's here."

Gina came in and smiled at Summer. "Hi! I'm glad you're back. How are you feeling? How's your voice?"

Summer nodded. "I'm great thanks, glad to be back. And now that I think about it, my voice is doing surprisingly well." She looked at Cassidy. "You haven't told me to shut up once today."

"You're right. I hadn't noticed till now, but you haven't croaked at all!"

Gina laughed. "Well, I guess that's good then."

"It's great," said Summer.

"Just don't go overdoing it," said Cassidy.

Summer rolled her eyes. "Yes, Mom!"

Cassidy shook her head. "Don't give me that! Just because I'm the responsible one and I care."

"You do make a good mom, though," said Gina. "Are you practicing for the real thing?"

Summer looked at her in surprise. Joking aside, she'd never thought of Cassidy as the maternal type. Her getting engaged to Shane was wonderful, but the thought of them having babies was a little surprising, to say the least.

Cassidy shook her head. "Not yet. Jesus, Gina, we're only just planning our engagement party. What about you? You're getting married in a couple of months, any baby plans for you?"

Gina shook her head. "No, not for a long while yet."

"When are you getting married?" asked Summer. "I'm behind on all the news. I only just found out about *her* engagement party." She jerked her head toward Cassidy. "She forgot to invite me."

"Well, you're invited to our wedding," said Gina. "I wouldn't forget you. Will you still be here by the end of August?"

Cassidy gave her a pointed look. "What do you think, will you be?"

Summer didn't know. Three months from now would take her to the middle of August. She didn't have to leave as soon as the time was up, but she also knew Cassidy's question was bigger than that. She was asking if Summer planned to return to her career at all. She didn't know the answer to that yet. "It doesn't matter either way. I'll come to the wedding no matter what."

"Good," said Gina. "We'd love you to be there."

Cassidy held Summer's gaze for a moment longer. She obviously had more to say, but to Summer's relief, she let it go. Who knew how things would stand by the end of August? So much could happen between now and then.

"I will be. Thanks for inviting me."

Gina smiled.

"Hadn't you better get going?" asked Cassidy. "You're not going to have much time if you want to get groceries and get home before your hot date tonight."

Summer nodded. "I'd better get going."

Gina raised an eyebrow at her. "Are you seeing Carter?"

"I am." She couldn't help the big smile that spread across her face as she said it.

Gina grinned back. "That's wonderful! I hope you have a great time."

"Thanks. I'm sure I will. I'll see you ladies soon." Her voice cracked halfway through and she finished on a whisper.

Cassidy shook her head. "You might want to see if you and Carter can do something that doesn't involve too much talking."

Summer laughed. "I'd love to. It's him you need to convince, not me!"

Gina laughed. "Don't hold your breath! You can expect a full and proper courtship from Carter. He's not the kind to rush you into bed."

Summer rolled her eyes. "So, I'm finding out! But what if *I* want to rush *him* into bed?"

Gina's expression sobered quickly. "I think you'd be better taking your time, Summer."

She nodded. She already knew it. She'd hate to scare him away by being too forward.

"Get going!" said Cassidy. "The only rushing you need to be doing right now is to the grocery store!"

"Okay, I'm going. See you soon."

Chapter Seven

Carter finished up his workout and headed for the locker room. He felt great. He'd almost skipped the gym so that he could head back down to Summer's place early, but the way his body kept reacting to the thought of a whole evening alone with her let him know that he had to burn off some energy somehow. He was startled when Melanie stepped out in front of him.

"Hi, Carter."

"Hello." Man, he could do without stopping to talk to her. She stood there smiling at him expectantly. What did she want? Then he remembered. She'd asked if he wanted to go out with her sometime and said he could take some time to think it over. Shit! He didn't know what to say.

"How are you?"

Damn, he didn't want to drag this out. "I'm good, thanks, but I'm in a bit of a hurry."

She looked so disappointed, he felt bad, but not bad enough to hang around. He darted for the locker room door and heaved a sigh of relief when it closed behind him. That had been pretty shitty of him, he thought as he collected his bag. He should have told her that he wasn't interested. It wasn't right of him to leave her hanging like that. He'd have to tell her straight away the next time he saw her. For now, he hurried to his truck because he wanted to see Summer—not because he wanted to escape from Melanie!

When he got home, he went out back to check on the cats. Buster was holding court in the shed with four of his buddies. They all came to rub around his legs in greeting. He smiled. He viewed them as his guilty secret—he could just imagine Beau's face if he knew he took such good care of a bunch of strays. He made a fuss over each of them before filling the food and water bowls he left out. He turned at the sound of mewing just outside the broken board. Squatting down to peer out, he saw a cat he didn't recognize. He went to open the door. As she came toward him, it was obvious why she hadn't come in the way the others did. She was heavily pregnant and wouldn't have fit through the gap. He held the door for her to come in. She just stood there and mewed up at him, but wouldn't come inside.

Damn. He couldn't leave her out. She looked like she could have her kittens at any minute. He came out and closed the door. She followed him across the yard back to the house. Great. She didn't want to have her kittens out in the shed, but she was happy to come into the house. He held the door open and she came inside. She sniffed around cautiously and then made her way to the laundry room. Carter followed and watched as she began to knead at the pile of towels on the floor. She lay down and purred up at him gratefully. Great! What was he supposed to do now? Call Summer and tell her he couldn't see her tonight because he needed to play midwife to a cat? He let out a little chuckle. Apparently he was going to have to do just that. He didn't see himself driving away and leaving this girl to do her thing in the laundry room all by herself. He'd never forgive himself if something went wrong. He fished his phone out of his back pocket while he went into the kitchen and brought a bowl of water. He dialed the number and waited.

"Hey, are you on the way?" asked Summer. Her voice sounded scratchy.

"Sorry, but I'm not."

"Oh." He couldn't help but smile. She sounded disappointed! "Is everything all right?"

"Everything's fine so far, but I need to stick around here to make sure that it stays that way."

"Why, what's going on?" She sounded genuinely concerned. Even to his own ears, his laugh sounded embarrassed. "Umm, I don't know what you're going to make of this, but I have cats. Well, I don't really have cats, they just kind of live around here, and I take care of them…"

"I love cats!"

He smiled. That was something, he supposed. Maybe she'd understand, then. "Well, you see, one of them has decided that tonight is the night she needs to have her kittens. She's made herself a nest in my laundry room. I don't want to leave her in case she needs me. I'm sorry."

There was a long silence before she spoke. Carter was starting to think he'd blown it. She must think he was an idiot! What kind of guy would pass up a date with Summer just so he could be there for a stray cat? When she eventually spoke, her words warmed his heart.

"Oh, Carter! That's awesome!"

"It is?" He wasn't totally sure whether she meant it. Maybe she was being sarcastic?

"It is! That's so sweet of you! Can I come? Can I help? Do you want me to bring anything?"

Carter grinned. That wasn't the reaction he'd been expecting, it was so much better than he'd dared hope for! "I'd love you to come, if you want to. I don't know that there's anything we can do. I'm sure she knows what she's doing. I just can't bring myself to leave her, in case she hits any problems."

"Of course not. Listen, I went to the grocery today. How about I bring a frozen pizza and a bottle of wine? We can still have dinner and we'll be there for her if she needs us."

"That sounds great. If you're sure you don't mind?"

"I don't mind at all! I'm on my way!"

"Okay, well drive safely. Watch out for deer."

"I will. See you soon."

Carter hung up and looked down at the cat who had curled up on top of the towels. "Okay, lady. I hope you know what you're doing, because I'm not sure I do." He didn't just mean that he'd never delivered kittens before. He also wondered what he was doing letting Summer come over to join him— with a bottle of wine—which meant she wouldn't be driving home tonight.

He'd worry about that when she got here. For now he wanted to make sure that he had everything he might need on hand. For a moment he stood and looked around the little laundry room. The cat looked as though she might be getting close. She was crouched on top of the pile of towels panting. He had no idea how long a labor might last. He took his phone back out. He was going to have to call Doc Lee. The old guy would no doubt be surprised to get a call about a cat, but he'd taken care of all the Remingtons' animals for as long as Carter could remember.

Once he hung up with the vet he smiled. He shouldn't have worried. Of course Doc Lee had told him everything he needed to know, everything he needed to look for, and when to call him if it looked like there were problems. He might be more used to assisting with breached calves or foals, but he cared just as much about little stray kittens. Carter busied himself in the kitchen making sure he'd have everything he needed, just in case. From what the Doc said, as long as things went well, the kitty would take care of everything herself.

He looked around, wondering what Summer would make of his place. It wasn't exactly a palace or even anything like the place she was staying in, but if it was enough to put her off him, then it was better that they both find that out now.

~ ~ ~

Summer was glad she'd bought one of those insulated bags that kept things frozen at the grocery store this afternoon. She slid the pizza inside along with a bottle of wine and a tub of ice cream. They had been her supplies for a quiet night at home; she would never have guessed that she'd be taking them up to Carter's place tonight. She also would never have guessed that her plans for the evening would have evolved from having Carter over to dinner, to going out with him to Chico, to this—heading up to his place with frozen pizza, and intending to assist in the delivery of kittens. She grinned as she grabbed the car keys and headed out the door. Just the thought of Carter—big, burly Carter—being so concerned about a momma kitty melted her insides. The fact that he would have stood her up in order to help a cat, made her grin like a crazy person. She hadn't really dated much over the last few years. It was hard. She never knew if guys were really interested in her or just interested in being seen with a country singer. None of the guys she had dated would have stood her up for a cat; she was pretty sure of that! It just added to Carter's charm. He was a one of a kind without a doubt! She threw the bag into the car and set out up the valley. As she drove, she couldn't stop smiling to herself. She might be thirty miles from town, but it was such a beautiful drive. She already loved this place. She loved the kind of life she got to live here. It felt so free, so real. Her smile faded. She'd love to make it last. To make this her real life. She'd love to trade her apartment in Nashville for the house on the river. Trade the concerts and studio sessions for nights out with Cassidy and her friends—and nights in with Carter! She shouldn't be thinking like that though. Tonight wouldn't be about a night in with him. It would be about taking care of a momma cat and her new kittens. How could she be thinking about sleeping with Carter? How could she not?

Half an hour later, she slowed as she crossed the river and came to the outskirts of town. She knew Carter's nursery was right there; she'd driven past it enough times. She turned into the driveway that led past the nursery itself and around to the house at the back. She'd never been able to see it properly from the road, sheltered as it was by a line of spruce. It was beautiful. A little wooden cottage. It looked as though it should be tucked away in the woods somewhere. She parked the car out front and sat there for a moment. This was Carter's home. It suited him. It looked functional and wasn't anything fancy, but it held a certain charm. She got out of the car and pulled the bag with the pizza out. She felt a little guilty as she looked at the other bag sitting on the passenger seat. It was a little overnight bag—just a change of clothes and her toothbrush, that was all. He hadn't invited her to stay; in fact, he hadn't invited her at all. She'd invited herself. But she couldn't exactly drive back down the valley at who-knew-what-time of night. Especially if they were going to get through that bottle of wine she'd brought. She decided to leave the bag there for now. It might seem a little presumptuous to show up on his doorstep with it.

She went up the steps to the front door and knocked. She looked around as she waited. There were planter boxes everywhere, of course. The front door opened and she caught her breath at the sight of him. He was shirtless! Again.

She grinned as she looked him over. "Well, hello!"

He chuckled. "Hello yourself. Sorry. Come on in. I had to get a quick shower before you got here. Come on through. I'll just go grab a shirt."

She smiled. "No hurry. I kind of like it."

He shook his head. "You must be getting used to it by now. I was bare chested this morning, same again now."

She laughed. "If I didn't know better I might think you were determined to show off all those muscles of yours!"

He smiled, but a hint of color touched his cheeks and he looked away. "Well, you do know better."

She touched his arm. "Yes, I do. And I'm sorry, but I can't hide it. I love seeing you like that."

He lifted his head and smiled. "I'm glad, but let's not stand here talking about it." He led her through to the kitchen. "Do you need to put anything in the fridge?"

She nodded. "Yeah, let me sort out what I brought while you go grab a shirt."

He gave her a grateful smile and disappeared upstairs.

Summer smiled as a little shiver ran through her. She couldn't help hoping that she'd be going up there with him later and helping him take the shirt back off... After pulling herself together, she put the ice cream in the freezer and stood the wine and the pizza on the counter. She looked at the oven, wondering whether she should turn it on to preheat. She decided not. First priority should be the cat—not her rumbling tummy. Instead she opened the drawers to look for a corkscrew. She was definitely ready for a glass of wine.

She poured two glasses and turned at the sound of Carter coming back downstairs. He stopped in the kitchen doorway and smiled at her. God, he was gorgeous! She smiled back and held out a glass to him.

"Thanks," he said as he took it. "Do you want to come meet our momma-to-be?"

"Yes, please. I didn't want to go and disturb her."

He led her down the hallway and held open the door to the laundry room. Summer peered around it and then smiled up at him. "She looks like she's nearly ready."

He nodded and stepped inside. "Doc Lee said to leave her to it as much as possible. I don't want to interfere. I just wanted to be here in case she needs us."

Summer nodded. "I'm sure she'll be fine."

The cat looked up and mewled between her panting.

Summer squatted down beside her. "You're going to be fine, little lady. You can do this, we're here." She reached her hand out for the cat to sniff. She did and then head butted her gently. "See," said Summer. "We're friends. We're here if you need us."

She looked up at Carter. The way he was looking at her made her breath catch in her chest. "What?"

He shook his head slowly. "When I called you to say I couldn't come, I thought you might be mad at me for putting a cat ahead of you. I had no need to worry, did I?"

She smiled. "None at all!"

"I thought you might think less of me."

Summer got to her feet and came to stand before him. "Then you don't know me very well, do you? I would have thought a hell of a lot less of you if you'd left her here by herself just so you could come see me."

He smiled. "I can see that now. Thank you."

"For what?"

He put a hand on her shoulder. "Just for being who you are."

That made her insides turn mushy. This gorgeous man was standing there, smiling down at her, his hand on her shoulder sending ripples of desire coursing through her, and he was thanking her just for being her! Did it get any better than this?

"Thank *you*, for being you," she replied.

He let out a little chuckle. "I guess neither of us can help being who we are, can we?"

She shook her head. "I guess not." Her stomach chose that moment to let out a loud gurgle.

Carter laughed. "And I guess we can't help being hungry either." He gave the cat an apologetic look. "You're going to have to manage by yourself for a minute while I get the oven going, kitty."

The cat seemed to understand his words and gave a frightened little mew.

"How about you stay here with her and I'll go put the pizza in?"

"You don't mind?" he asked.

"Of course I don't." It seemed as though the cat was already attached to Carter and was looking to him for reassurance. Summer was happy to make herself useful in the kitchen. She had to smile as Carter squatted down on the floor and the cat rubbed her head against him. He was so gentle for such a big guy. "I'll be back," she said.

She looked around the kitchen. It was well laid out, neat and well organized. She'd always thought a kitchen told a lot about a person. This one said that Carter was no slob. She turned on the oven to preheat and checked the cabinets for a cookie sheet. She had to smile. Apparently he was no cook either. She found a cookie sheet, along with a whole set of pans and bakeware that looked as though they'd never been used. They were, however, neatly stacked.

Once the oven was ready, she slid the pizza in and set the timer, then made her way back to the laundry room. She smiled at the sight of Carter sitting on the floor leaning back against the washer as he sipped his wine. He looked up when she came in.

"I think she's nearly ready."

As if to confirm his assessment, the cat meowed and started to push. Summer watched in amazement as the first kitten came into the world. She felt tears sting her eyes as she watched the new mother lick her tiny baby clean and it wriggled blindly against her.

Carter looked up at her—it seemed his eyes were shining, too. "Wow!" was all he said.

Summer grinned at him. "Wow, is right!"

He reached up to take hold of her hand and she sat down on the floor beside him.

"Doc said it could be up to half an hour between each kitten."

Summer looked at the cat who seemed to be getting to ready to go again. She raised an eyebrow. "I don't think it'll take that long for this one."

She was right. Within a few minutes the second kitten appeared. She grinned up at Carter and he grinned back. She loved that he seemed as awestruck as she felt. They were witnessing one of life's miracles and she was so glad they got to share it. She watched the cat lick her second baby clean.

"What's her name?"

Carter shook his head. "I'm sure she doesn't have one. I've never seen her around before tonight. What do you think we should call her?"

Summer looked at her. She was a dark tabby. "I don't know. I want to call her hero right now. But that's not really a girl's name, is it?"

Carter smiled. "It should be. I think it suits her."

The cat looked up at him and meowed.

"What do you think then, Hero?"

She meowed again.

"I guess she likes it," said Summer. "Hero it is."

The timer on the oven dinged.

"I'll go get it," she said. "Should I just bring it in here?"

"Yes, please. I'm starving, but I don't want to leave her. I have no idea how many more kittens there are to come."

Summer sliced the pizza and brought the whole thing in. She put the plate up on top of the washer and handed Carter a slice wrapped in a paper towel.

"Thanks."

They munched in silence, watching Hero with her two babies. After a while, Carter turned to her with a rueful smile. "Some first date, huh?"

Summer laughed. "It's certainly an unusual first date. I've never had one quite like this before."

He looked sad. "There I go, falling below standard as usual. I'll make it up to you."

She smiled up at him. "This isn't *below* standard! This is so much better! There's nothing to make up for."

He didn't look convinced.

"Oh, I think there may be another one coming!" They both watched as Hero crouched again. "How many do you think there are?"

"I don't know," replied Carter. "Doc Lee said a standard litter is maybe three to five kittens." He shrugged. "I don't know the first thing about her. How old she is or if this is her first litter. I guess we just have to wait and see."

This time seemed more difficult. Hero mewled and panted and seemed to be pushing, but nothing was happening. Summer gave Carter a worried look. "Do you think we need to do anything?"

He shook his head. "Give her time. She'll get there."

Summer felt bad for the poor thing as she continued to pant and heave. After what seemed like ages, a third kitten appeared.

"Thank goodness!" she smiled up at Carter, but he still looked concerned.

She watched as the little thing lay there—still. Hero didn't immediately go to lick it. Oh, no! She looked up at Carter again. He shook his head and held a hand out to stop her as Summer went to reach out. "Give her a minute."

Summer held her breath. Hero lay still, panting and showing no interest in her latest arrival. Surely they had to do something. She let her breath out in a big sigh when Carter got up and washed his hands. He gently scooped up the lifeless little body and removed the membrane that still covered its face. Summer and Hero both watched him. The kitten still showed no sign of life. He shook his head sadly and sat back down. Summer watched through a blur of tears as he held the little thing face down and ran a finger over its chest. It seemed to sputter and a tiny trickle of liquid came out of its nose. Then it let out a little mew. That sparked Hero's interest. Carter placed the kitten beside her and she began to lick it.

Summer wiped her eyes and grinned at Carter. "Now *you're* the hero!"

His eyes were glistening as he grinned back. "Thank God for that!"

She nodded. "Thank Carter for that. You saved it!"

He nodded and looked at Hero who was now nursing her little ones. "I just helped. I hope that's all of them."

Summer nodded. So did she. She didn't think her nerves could take that again. They sat there for a long while watching the new momma clean herself and her babies up. She looked to be done.

Carter looked at Summer. "What do you think, shall we leave her to it?"

She nodded. "I guess." She looked at the forgotten pizza sitting on top of the washer. "Do you want me to reheat that while you wash up?"

"Please." He held up his empty glass. "And I think we both deserve more wine, don't you?"

"I do."

A little while later they settled in the living room. Summer sipped her wine and watched Carter eat his pizza. He stopped and looked up at her. "Is everything okay?"

"Couldn't be better. I'm just thinking how wonderful you are."

He grinned. "Thanks. But why?"

She laughed. "Because you are. What you did tonight."

"You would have done it if I wasn't there."

"I don't just mean with that last kitten. I mean bringing her into the house in the first place. Being prepared to cancel our date."

He shrugged. "I had to do that. If you didn't understand, then there wouldn't be a lot of point in us seeing each other at all, would there?"

She knew what he meant. "No, there wouldn't. But you were worried I might not understand, weren't you?"

He nodded. "I guess I was. But what matters is that you *did* understand. We took care of her, and now there are three new little kittens in the world."

Summer raised her glass. "There are. Here's to three little kittens."

Carter chinked his glass against hers. "Three little kittens."

When they'd finished eating they went to check on them. Summer peered around the door and smiled. The babies were sleeping nestled into their momma. She raised her head and looked up at them. She looked exhausted.

Carter put a bowl of food a little ways away from her and pulled the door most of the way closed. "I guess what they need now is rest." He looked at Summer. "I guess we do, too."

Summer looked at the kitchen clock. It was almost midnight. "I should go."

He cocked his head to one side and gave her a knowing smile. "You're not going anywhere. You know full well I wouldn't let you drive home at this hour, especially not with a couple of glasses of wine in you."

She smiled. She'd said it automatically, but she had no intention of getting behind the wheel of a car tonight. "Do you mind if I stay?"

He smiled. "I don't mind at all. I want you to."

Her smile grew wider. Now, they were getting somewhere. "I have to admit I have a bag in the car."

He shook his head at her. "Well then why don't you go get it? I'll see you upstairs."

Summer almost skipped on her way to collect her bag. She wanted him so badly! And it seemed he wasn't going to offer any more resistance. He was waiting for her upstairs. She grabbed her bag and had to stop herself from running up the stairs to find him.

"In here," he called when she reached the landing. She followed the sound of his voice. His bedroom was cozy. The furniture was made of logs, there was a fireplace in the corner, and he'd been setting a fire there. How romantic!

He grinned at her. "I wanted to make sure it was comfy in here for you."

"It's lovely. Thank you." She stepped toward him, but he backed away.

"I'll be across the landing."

She frowned, not sure she understood.

"In the spare room."

"Oh!"

He chuckled. "Don't look at me like that. I told you, we're not going to rush it. I'm not the kind to sleep with someone on a first date—and we haven't even been on our first date yet."

"But…" She was disappointed, but not really surprised. She gave him a rueful smile. "Okay. I'll see you in the morning, I guess."

He put his big hands on her shoulders and dropped a sweet kiss on her lips. "You will. Good night, Summer."

"Good night." She sighed as he closed the door behind him.

Chapter Eight

The next morning Carter tried not to make too much noise while he fixed the coffee. He'd had a restless night to say the least. After he'd said good night to Summer he'd gone to bed in the spare room, but hadn't been able to go to sleep. He'd lain there staring up at the ceiling wondering if he was crazy. He'd passed up on a date with her in order to deliver kittens, and then he'd let her stay the night, in his bed, and he'd let her sleep alone. She was lying feet away from him. He'd put money on him being the only guy in the world who wouldn't be in bed with her. He'd tossed and turned and eventually got up and gone down to check on Hero and her babies. She'd looked up at him with an expression on her face that looked a lot like gratitude. Maybe he was just kidding himself, but it sure looked like it. He hated to think what would have happened if he had gone out and left her to deliver by herself. He was pretty sure there would only be two kittens lying beside her.

He went and popped his head around the laundry room door while the coffee brewed. The kittens were nursing. He left them to it. He was happy to have been able to help, but he didn't want to interfere. He didn't think momma would want to stick around for long and he didn't want her or the little ones becoming dependent on him if they were going to go back out in the world and have to fend for themselves. He shook his head as he pulled the door to. He did know that if she wanted to stick around, he'd gladly let her. Buster and his buddies had made the shed their home, but that had been their choice. Carter would have let them in the house if that's what they'd wanted.

He cocked his head to one side at the sound of movements upstairs. Summer was up and about then. He poured himself a coffee and set a mug out ready for her. He'd already decided that he was going to take the morning off—maybe the whole day. He was almost finished over at Cassidy's place. He'd told the guys they could take off early for the weekend. It wasn't like him to skip work. But then it wasn't like him to be wanting to spend time with a woman either.

He smiled when she came into the kitchen. She was so damned beautiful. What kind of crazy was he that he kept refusing to sleep with her?

"Good morning," she said with a smile. "How's our new momma and the little ones?"

He loved that Hero and her kittens were Summer's first concern. That said a lot about her in his book.

"They're doing great. Do you want to come see?"

She nodded and followed him to peek around the laundry room door. "Aww. Aren't they adorable?"

He nodded. They really were. "Do you want coffee?"

"I'd love some, please."

Once she had her mug, they sat at the table in the breakfast nook.

Summer checked her watch. "I'm sorry. Am I making you late? Do you need me to get going?"

"No. I wondered if you want to go out for breakfast?"

Her smile lit up her face. "I'd love to. Don't you need to go to work though?"

"No. It's fine." He was going to make an excuse, say it was a quiet day or something, but he thought better of it, deciding instead to be honest. "I probably should, but I don't want to. I'd rather spend the time with you."

His honesty was rewarded with the biggest smile he'd seen on her face yet. "Thank you!"

He shook his head—she was thanking *him?* Surely that should be the other way around? "I thought we could go to Pine Creek. They do a great breakfast."

"That sounds wonderful."

Half an hour later, Carter pulled up in the parking lot at Pine Creek. Despite having told Summer that they did a great breakfast, he hadn't actually been here in years. He knew his parents liked to eat here on Sunday mornings when they could, so it must be good—he hoped.

He came around and opened Summer's door for her. She slid down and smiled up at him. "Who'd have thought our first real date would turn out to be breakfast?"

He smiled back, wondering who would ever believe him that he was taking her out for breakfast, after she'd spent the night at his place, and he still hadn't slept with her?

Inside, the hostess greeted them with a smile. "Carter! It's good to see you in here. And…" She did a double take as she looked at Summer and obviously recognized her. "Oh! It's good to see you, too. Welcome. Will it be a table for two?"

Carter nodded. Grateful that she didn't seem to be about to make a fuss.

"How about a corner table?"

"That'd be great, thanks."

They followed her. The place was quiet, just a few tables were occupied and she led them to the very far corner away from the others. She turned to them with a conspiratorial smile. "Is this okay?"

"Thank you. This is wonderful. We do appreciate it," said Summer.

Carter smiled. It was perfect. He'd been a little nervous on the drive over here as to whether they would get to eat in peace, or whether Summer would be recognized.

Once they were settled, Jean—he remembered her name now—brought them coffee and menus. "The special is the eggs benedict." She smiled at Summer. "But if there's anything you want that isn't on the menu, you just say so. We'll be glad to make whatever you'd like." She looked over her shoulder, as if to check no one was listening. "We're thrilled to have you here. Anything you want, you just let me know."

Summer smiled back at her. "Thank you. I'd love the eggs benedict, please."

"Coming right up," said Jean. "And you, Carter? Do you need a minute?"

"I'll do the same."

Once she'd gone, he smiled at Summer. "Is it like this everywhere you go?"

"Not at all. This is wonderful. She's so nice." She shrugged. "Sometimes people make a big fuss and I wish I'd stayed at home. Other times people make a big deal of not saying anything, but they nudge each other and whisper, and that gets pretty uncomfortable too. This is just perfect."

Carter was glad. He'd hate for her to feel uncomfortable.

She sipped on her coffee and smiled at him. He wanted to pinch himself. Was he really sitting here having breakfast with Summer Breese?

"Do you have any plans this weekend?" she asked. "I was thinking I'd like to go down to the park and have a look around."

His heart sank. He'd promised Mason that he'd help him with the horses. Family came first, without question, but right now, he was wishing he hadn't said yes.

Summer's smile faded. He must have been quiet too long.

He didn't want her getting the idea that he didn't want to spend time with her. "I'd love to go with you, but I need to help Mason at the ranch."

"I see."

He had the feeling that she really didn't see. "You could come with me if you like? We're working in some of the horses. You could watch? Though I don't know how much fun that'll be. We could head on down to the park when we're done."

Her smile returned. "I'd love to watch."

He nodded. He hoped Mason wouldn't mind.

Jean returned with their food, making Carter smile. Although his parents liked to eat here, his mom always complained about how slow the service was. He should tell her to come with Summer if she wanted to speed things up.

"Can I get you anything else?"

"This is great, thank you," said Summer with a smile. "It looks wonderful!"

Jean was obviously pleased with the compliment. Carter loved that Summer wanted to make her feel good. She definitely wasn't one of those celebrities who was difficult or demanding.

While they were eating, a couple came in and Jean led them to the other side of the restaurant, seating them as far away from Carter and Summer as she could. He noticed that it didn't stop them from glancing over every now and then. He hoped they weren't going to come over. He was enjoying this and didn't want any intrusions.

Summer grinned at him as she finished her food. "That was wonderful!"

He grinned back. "It doesn't look like there's anything wrong with your appetite."

She shrugged. "I enjoy my food. I always have. Though I must admit I'm used to at least getting on the treadmill every day to work it off." She raised an eyebrow at him. "I don't suppose you feel like taking me to your gym, do you?"

He nodded slowly, uncertain as to what kind of reception she might receive there.

She looked a little disappointed and he realized that this might look like the second time in ten minutes that she was asking to do something with him and he was being less than enthusiastic in his response.

He smiled. "Hey, don't get me wrong. I'd love to. I just don't know if the guys in there would know how to behave themselves around you."

She smiled back. "That's okay. I'm sure you can protect me. I'm just glad it's the guys you're worried about and not the girls."

He gave her a puzzled look.

She laughed. "For a minute there I had visions of you not wanting to upset all your female admirers by taking me in with you."

He had to laugh at that. "I don't have any female admirers."

"I don't believe you for a minute! I'll bet you do really, don't you? You're not trying to tell me that there isn't a woman in there who follows you around begging you to go out with her, are you?"

His smile faded as he remembered Melanie.

~ ~ ~

Summer's smile faded too. "Oh!"

"No! It's not like that. I've been working out in there for years. I've never been interested in the ladies and they've never been interested in me."

She gave him a skeptical look.

"It's true! They know I'm not in the market, so they don't bother." He sighed. "Well, they didn't. Until you. They realized that I might be back in the market, so there's one girl who wants me to take her out, but I'm not going to."

Summer felt bad. She'd felt a momentary jealousy and had only intended to tease him. She was pretty much convinced there were quite a few women who were interested in Carter. How could there not be? He was gorgeous looking and a genuinely good guy. She hadn't meant to make him uncomfortable, and she certainly hadn't intended to make herself feel uncomfortable about some nameless girl at the gym who might be her competition for Carter's affection. She couldn't help wondering now, if *she* might be the reason that Carter didn't want to sleep with her? Maybe he was keeping his options open?

He held her gaze. "What are you thinking?"

She shook her head. "That I wish I'd kept my mouth shut. I was only teasing, but now I feel jealous."

Carter laughed. "Do you realize how ridiculous that sounds?"

She sighed. "Probably. But that just makes me feel stupid."

"Oh, darlin', I'm sorry." He reached across the table and took hold of her hand.

She couldn't help but smile at the way his huge hand engulfed hers. She met his gaze and squeezed. "Please don't be. It's just me being silly. I like you. I know lots of other women must like you, too. I'm just a visitor, I'm an oddity. I know that…"

He held her gaze. "You're special is what you are. You'll have to forgive me. I didn't mean to make you feel bad. It's just the thought of *you* being jealous over *me* seems a little far-fetched. You know? You're the big country star. I'm just the yard guy. The guy at the gym."

She shook her head firmly. "No. Look at it from my perspective for a minute, would you. I am the country singer, I'll give you that, and that might seem great from the outside. But from where I sit, it's not so great at all. It means I don't get to be me. I don't get to ever have anyone care about me just because I'm me. I get guys who want to date the country singer, but who never know or care who I really am or what I want…"

"But I…" Carter started to interrupt, but she held a hand up to stop him.

"Exactly. I know! You're not like that. You like me, you care about me, you couldn't care less that I sing or that people know me. That's why it matters so much to me. You're amazing, and part of me thinks that you're too amazing to want to get caught up in the circus that is my life. You're genuine and you're real and that makes you more likely to want a girl who works out at the gym with you, than to want me. And that's what makes me jealous!" Her voice was raspy by the time she'd finished. That was a lot to say in one go, but she'd needed to say it—for her own sake as well as Carter's. She was getting clear about how she felt. He *thought* that she was the prize, just because she had some silly singing career, and all the money and fame that went with it. She *knew* that, in fact, he was the prize, and not just because he didn't care about any of that!

He stared at her for a long moment.

"Sorry," she said. "Sorry, I ranted at you, and sorry that I got jealous."

His slow smile spread across his face and he relaxed. "No, I'm sorry. I didn't mean to make you jealous." He pursed his lips and looked away for a moment.

"What?"

He looked back at her with a smile. "I kind of like it though."

She laughed, relieved.

He was looking away again. She followed his gaze. The couple who had just come in kept looking over at them. She sighed. She shouldn't expect to escape from prying eyes completely.

"Do you want to leave?" asked Carter.

"I don't. I want to sit here with you and enjoy the rest of my coffee. They don't mean any harm, I'm sure they're just curious."

"Okay. Whatever you want. But we can go if they make you uncomfortable."

"I'm fine." She had a feeling Carter was more uncomfortable than she was.

"What do you want to do next?" he asked.

"Do I get you for the whole day?"

He nodded. "If you want me."

She couldn't help laughing. "You know I do. But apparently we're not allowed to go there—yet!"

He laughed with her. "You know what I mean."

"And you know what I mean, too. Do you think we should go back and check on momma and her kittens before we do anything else?"

"Yeah. I'd like to."

"Let's do that then."

"Okay, and then how about I take you out to the ranch? If we go have a quick look around now, you'll be better able to decide if you want to spend any time there this weekend. I'd hate for you to feel you're stuck there for hours if you don't like it."

She smiled. He was so sweet. "I'd love to go see, but I'm not worried about not liking it. I'm sure I'll love it. I used to ride growing up. I love horses and being around them."

He smiled at that. "Okay then, let's get out of here." He caught Jean's attention, which wasn't hard to do, since she seemed to have been hovering unobtrusively the whole time. Once he'd paid they made their way to the door. Summer was acutely aware of the couple seated by the windows watching them. She nodded and gave a friendly smile as they passed. They smiled back and that was it. What a relief!

Chapter Nine

Carter brought the truck to a stop outside the barn. He'd called ahead to let Mason know that he was bringing Summer down for a look around.

She jumped out before he had chance to go around and get her door for her. He crammed his hat on his head and went around to stand beside her.

"Oh, Carter, I love it! This place is amazing."

"I'm glad you think so. I'm kind of partial to it myself."

"I can see why. How lucky were you that you got to grow up here!"

He nodded. He did consider himself lucky. He looked around, trying to see the place through new eyes. Through Summer's eyes. How must it look? He had to admit the ranch was pretty impressive. They'd come down the long driveway from the road, past the big house, which stood on a little rise. It was a two story with a wraparound porch. He was pretty sure his mom had popped out onto the porch for a second when they'd passed, too. They'd stopped here in front of the barn which was pretty impressive in its own right. On the other side of the driveway was the entrance to Shane's guest ranch. The lodge was hidden from sight, but the first few cabins were in view. As he looked over at them, Carter realized that for the first time, he felt no pain. He'd lived in the end cabin—it had been the only cabin in those days—with Trisha when they got married. He'd come home to that cabin to find her in bed with one of the hands. Every time he'd seen the place in the years since that day, he'd felt a mixture of pain and shame. He was ashamed that he hadn't been enough for her. Ashamed that he'd been too stupid to know what was going on. Ashamed that his heartbreak had been so public. It was odd to him that today, for the first time, he felt nothing.

Summer put a hand on his arm and smiled up at him.

Was she the reason? And was she going to be the cause of even more pain?

"Are you going to show me around?" she asked.

"Yeah. Come on. Let's start in the barn."

Mason met them at the doors. He slapped Carter's shoulder. "Good to see you." He tipped his hat to Summer. "And you. How are you settling back in?"

Summer smiled. "Wonderfully, thank you." She shot a look at Carter. "Though that's mostly to do with your brother, here."

Carter felt the color in his cheeks. Damn. He wished he could somehow make himself stop doing that. He didn't feel too bad though. It made him happy that Summer was open about liking him. It made him happy that she was interested in seeing his life. He wasn't going to let himself worry about how he'd feel when she'd gone. If he was smart, he might not want to let her into every part of his life—but then no one had ever accused him of being smart.

Mason grinned at them both. "Well, if you guys are busy this weekend, don't worry about me, Carter. I can take care of the McClellan horses no problem."

Carter was tempted to say, great. But he couldn't bring himself to leave Mason in the lurch. Summer took the decision away from him, anyway.

"I'm excited to come watch," she said. "If I'm not going to be in the way."

"Not at all," said Mason. He looked up and grinned when he saw their mom approaching. Carter pursed his lips. Would it be too much to ask that he should be able to take Summer to meet her when he was ready? Apparently it would. His mom reached them and smiled at Summer.

"Well, hello. How lovely to see you out here. I hope my boys are taking good care of you?"

Summer nodded. "They are thank you, Mrs. Remington. It's so nice to meet you."

Carter watched as his mom leaned in to hug her. She winked at him over Summer's shoulder. "I've been looking forward to meeting you, too. I won't keep you though. I just wanted to catch Mason here."

Mason shot Carter a look. They both knew she'd have called him if she just wanted to talk to him. "I guess I'll see you guys tomorrow then," said Mason. He jerked his head toward the barn. "Go say hi, if you like. The McClellan horses are out the back, but Jake and Lola are in there."

Carter nodded.

Mason took his mom's arm and started steering her back up to the house. She looked back over her shoulder at Summer. "So nice to meet you, my dear. I'll see you soon."

"I hope so," called Summer.

Carter led her into the barn.

"Who are Jake and Lola?" she asked.

Carter stopped in front of one of the stalls and smiled at his old friend. "This…" he held his hand out and the big gray gelding came to nuzzle his fingers "…is my best friend, Jake." Summer stood on tiptoe to peer over the stall door. "Oh, he's gorgeous!"

Carter laughed. "I guess that puts me in my place; you said the same thing about me!"

She laughed and pushed at his arm. "In a different way."

Jake came toward her and nibbled her hair. "Hello, handsome." She rubbed his nose. "It's nice to meet you. Is he yours?" she asked Carter.

He nodded. "We've been together since I was a kid. I took him with me when I moved up to town, but he hated it. He belongs down here on the ranch. I need to get out to see him more."

"Do you still ride him?"

"Not as often as I'd like to, but yeah. I take him out when I can."

Summer's eyes shone as she looked up at him. "Do you think I could go out with you sometime?"

"I'd love that. I think that's why Mason mentioned Lola. Come on, you should meet her."

He walked a few stalls further down and stopped. "How you doing, old girl?"

Lola came and leaned her head over the door and nickered gently. Summer rubbed her nose. "She's beautiful!"

Carter chuckled. "You're not doing my ego much good, you know. I thought it was just me, but you seem to fall in love with *every* animal you meet."

Summer's eyes widened as she stared at him.

Damn! He hadn't meant *fall in love*! He'd just meant that she thought they were all good looking, that her compliments to him were only the same as she paid to the horses. He stared back at her, stuck for words.

She smiled. "Your ego should be flattered. I just know good-looking when I see it, no matter what form it takes."

Carter watched gratefully as she patted Lola's cheek. "And this lady is a real looker. Aren't you, beautiful?"

She really was a good looking mare. She was a palomino, with a long silky mane, and huge, soft brown eyes.

"She's as sweet and gentle as she is beautiful, too," said Carter. Thinking as he did that she and Summer were a perfect match. "If you really do want to come out, you can ride her. She'll take great care of you."

"I'd love to. Thank you."

He looked up at the sound of footsteps entering the barn. A little girl came running toward them, startling him.

"Summer Breese!" she cried, then flung herself at Summer.

She was obviously more used to this than Carter was. She scooped the little thing up and gave her a hug. "That's me. And who might you be, young lady?"

"I'm Ruby. Will you sing for me?"

Carter had to smile. The kid was maybe five or six years old, all blonde curls and big blue eyes. She was kitted out in a checkered shirt, denims and cute little cowboy boots. He had to wonder where the hell she'd come from.

A couple came hurrying in after her. "Ruby!" called the woman.

Carter recognized them as the couple who'd been at Pine Creek this morning. He hoped to hell they hadn't followed Summer out here.

The guy shot them an apologetic look and the woman reached her arms out to the little girl. The kid wrapped her arms tightly around Summer's neck and shook her head.

"Ruby!"

"I'm so sorry about this," said the guy.

"It's okay," said Summer. "Ruby and I are just making friends."

"And Summer Breese is going to sing a song for me!"

"No, Ruby. I'm not. I can't at the moment. I have to rest my voice."

"Oh. Are you all right?"

Carter loved the way Summer smiled at the kid as she put her back down on the ground. "I'm fine, thank you, but I've done a lot of singing for a long time, and my voice needs a rest."

The woman took hold of the little girl's hand. "I'm so sorry."

Carter relaxed a little. It wasn't as though they'd come here to harass Summer. But still, he had to wonder. "What are you doing out here?" he asked.

"We're staying at the ranch," replied the guy.

The kid nodded. "Aunt Carly and Uncle James brought me to see the horses." She looked at Summer. "My mommy needs a rest, too. She doesn't sing though. She just has to work a lot."

Carter smiled. The kid was cute as a button.

"We'll leave you in peace," said the guy. "Sorry."

"It's fine," said Summer. "It was nice to meet you, Ruby."

"Are you staying here, too?"

"No. I just came out to see the horses."

"Will I see you again?"

Summer smiled. "Maybe."

"Come on, Ruby. We have to go."

"Bye!"

Carter had to chuckle as he watched them walk away. The kid kept looking back over her shoulder and waving. "Sorry about that," he said when they were out of earshot.

She shrugged. "It's hardly your fault, is it? And besides, as far as meeting fans out in public goes, that was one of my easier encounters."

Carter hated to think what some of the more difficult ones might be like. "Do you want to ride this afternoon?"

She shook her head. "I did, but I think I'd rather go home now."

His heart sank.

"If you want to hang out?" she added with a smile.

"I do. Let's get out of here."

~ ~ ~

Once they got back to Summer's place they sat out on the deck. "What would you normally do on a Friday afternoon?" she asked. Seeing him out at the barn, learning he still had a horse that he rode, and that he helped out at the ranch, she'd realized that she knew very little about his life. In fact other than his landscaping business and the fact that he spent a lot of time at the gym, she knew very little *about* him at all—even though she felt she knew *him* very well.

"Normally I'd be working."

"And then what?"

He shrugged. "I'd hit the gym. Go home. Have dinner. Read." He gave her a wry smile. "Hang out with the cats. I don't exactly lead a very exciting life."

"It sounds wonderful to me."

"Why, what would you normally do on a Friday afternoon and evening?"

"It depends. Sometimes I have to show up at places, you know, be seen out on the town in Nashville. If I'm on the road, then I'd be getting ready to go on stage. If I get my own way—which doesn't happen very often—I'd be curled up on the sofa at home in my PJs, reading a book, or eating ice cream and watching a sappy movie."

He laughed. "And here was I thinking you'd be out clubbing and partying till dawn."

She shook her head. "That's not me. I don't enjoy it. And besides, I turn back into a pumpkin at midnight. That's my absolute limit. I start yawning around eleven."

"I'm taking notes here. So no keeping you out late?"

"No," she waggled her eyebrows at him. "You have to get me home to bed early."

The heated look he gave her told her she might be wearing down his resolve. Well, good! She wasn't one to rush into bed with a guy, but they'd known each other for quite a while now. They were going somewhere together. Wherever that might be, she didn't see any reason to keep on waiting.

"Do you have any sappy movies here?"

She nodded. "There's a whole collection of them in the entertainment center. Beau has this place well stocked with everything, right down to movies to watch on a rainy day."

Carter looked out the window. It had indeed started to rain. "So how about we do that? Just curl up watch movies and have some down time. After all, you *are* supposed to be here to rest."

Summer couldn't think of anything she'd rather do than spend the evening curled up with him. "That sounds perfect. How about you choose a movie and I'll go get the ice cream?"

He chuckled. "You can't watch a movie without ice cream?"

She shook her head. "I could. But it wouldn't be nearly as enjoyable."

"Fair enough. What kind of movie do you want?"

"Surprise me." She was curious to know what he might choose.

When she came back into the living room, he was sitting on one end of the sofa. She plonked herself down beside him and handed him a bowl of ice cream.

He took it with a smile. "Thanks. I picked out a comedy, is that okay?"

"That's great." It would be good to laugh with him.

They sat side by side, eating their ice cream. It felt so natural, so comfortable. Summer was hoping to snuggle against him once the ice cream was gone. But even this, sitting here in companionable silence, watching the movie, felt wonderful. It just seemed so right. Carter was such a big, solid, reassuring presence. They didn't need to talk. With him, just being was enjoyable in itself.

Carter emptied his bowl and put it on the coffee table. When Summer finished, he took both bowls to the kitchen. When he came back and sat down again Summer couldn't resist. She snuggled into his side. He smiled down at her and wrapped his big arm around her shoulders. The way he gave her a squeeze was more of a friendly gesture than anything else, but it still set her heart racing.

She rested her head against his chest and lay her arm across his stomach with a smile. She let out a big sigh when he began to stroke her hair. Did it get any better than this? He smoothed her hair away from her forehead and peered down at her.

"You okay down there?"

"More than okay. I'm happy."

His slow smile spread across his face. "Me too." He leaned back against the sofa and continued to play with her hair.

Summer smiled to herself as she stared at the TV. She couldn't claim to be watching, she was too busy enjoying just being. Enjoying the feel of Carter. She couldn't remember ever feeling like this before. She was relaxed, happy, and comfortable. And it was all down to this big, beautiful man.

The next thing she knew, she was opening her eyes as Carter slid out from under her. She rubbed her eyes and looked up at him. "Where are you going?"

"I have to pee! Sorry I disturbed you, but I waited as long as I could. I have to pee and then I'd better get going."

"No!"

He chuckled. "We can argue about it in a minute."

Summer sat up and watched him disappear into the guest bathroom. Poor guy. She didn't know how long she'd been sleeping, but the movie was over and it was fully dark outside. He came back and sat down beside her. "I really don't want to argue about it. You know part of me wants to stay, but it's best if I go."

"But…"

He held up a hand. "I want to check on the kittens. I need to get my stuff together to go out to the ranch tomorrow." He smiled. "And I don't want to rush."

Summer sighed. "I'd hardly call it rushing anymore. Don't you think you've made me wait long enough already?"

He chuckled. "Maybe, but I couldn't relax if I stayed anyway. I really do need to check on the cats."

"I could come with you?" she asked hopefully.

He shook his head. "You need to rest. Go to bed. Get some sleep. I'll pick you up in the morning."

Summer stood up and reached her arms up around his neck. "Okay. You win. But will you come tuck me in before you go?"

His arms tightened around her, pulling her against him. "I don't think that's a good idea."

She pressed her hips against his, hoping to persuade him otherwise. "Please?"

He dropped a gentle peck on her lips before taking a step back. "Tomorrow."

Summer knew she was grinning like an idiot. "Tomorrow? You mean…" She didn't know what words to use, how to ask if he really meant that tomorrow he was finally going to give in and sleep with her!

He smiled at her through pursed lips. "I mean tomorrow I'll tuck you in."

She raised an eyebrow. "Before you leave?"

He shrugged and turned to make his way to the front door. "Maybe."

Chapter Ten

Carter reined in the mare he'd been putting through her paces. She was a sweetheart. She'd done everything he'd asked of her, and hadn't flinched at any of Mason's props. He dismounted and led her over to where Summer was perched on the fence to watch.

"She certainly looks like she's ready to me!"

Carter grinned. "She is. She did great."

Mason rode out into the arena on the next horse. He tipped his hat at them. "I can finish up here if you two want to get going."

Carter didn't want to leave his brother to work by himself, but he didn't want to leave Summer sitting around watching all day either. She'd been a great sport, but he was worried she might be getting bored. It was midafternoon now and she'd been hanging around since nine this morning. He gave her a questioning look.

She shook her head vigorously. "I don't want to leave. I'm loving watching."

He wasn't sure how true that was, but he was grateful that she seemed to understand him, and to understand his motivation. "You're sure?"

"I am." She smiled at Mason. "If you don't mind me hanging around?"

Mason grinned back. "Not at all."

Carter took the mare back into the barn and saddled up the next. Mason had done a great job of bombproofing them. He doubted there'd be any problems with them at all, but he understood the need to put them all through their paces one more time, just to be sure. He led the mare out into the sunlight and swung himself up into the saddle. If he was honest, he was enjoying himself. It'd been far too long since he'd ridden at all, let alone helped Mason out. The fact that Summer was perched on the fence, watching with an admiring smile on her face, made this all the more enjoyable.

He walked the mare over to the first obstacle Mason had set up—a row of poles with flags waving from them, and she didn't bat an eyelid. Next, he trotted her up to the row of tree trunks and urged her to step over them; again, she happily obliged.

He looked over at Summer. She had company now. The couple from yesterday and the little girl were standing chatting with her. He frowned. He didn't want them intruding. He trotted over to join them with a grim smile on his face. When he reached them, Summer let him know with her eyes that it was okay. He gave her the slightest nod before he spoke.

"Afternoon."

"Hi," said the woman "Sorry. We didn't mean to get in the way. We're just waiting for Beau."

That puzzled him. What might Beau want with them? And where was he? It wasn't like him to keep people waiting.

"He's taking us to view a couple of properties," explained the guy.

"Uncle James and Auntie Carla want to buy a house here," explained Ruby. Hers was the only name Carter had remembered. She grinned at Summer. "And when they do. I can come see Summer Breese whenever I like."

"Ruby!"

Summer laughed. "That's okay. I might see you sometimes."

"You live here, too, don't you?"

Summer met Carter's gaze. "Not exactly."

Carter's heart sank. No, she didn't exactly live here, did she? She was just visiting. And soon enough she'd be gone. He looked up to watch Beau's truck approach. "Here's your ride," he said. He turned the mare and headed back to the course. He didn't understand it, but his smile had evaporated. He just wanted to get away from the people who had just reminded him that he shouldn't be feeling so damned happy. He might be enjoying Summer's company, but he needed to remember that it was just a short-lived fantasy. It might be great while it lasted, but he was going to have to pay dearly with his heart when she left.

He watched from under the brim of his hat as Beau joined the little group by the fence. He shouldn't feel that way, but he resented those people. He resented that they were going to be moving here, when Summer wasn't.

~ ~ ~

Summer watched Carter ride the mare into the water. Why had he just ridden away like that? It wasn't like him to be rude to people. She had to wonder what had upset him.

"Hey folks." Beau grinned as he came to join them. He really was a good-looking guy when he smiled like that.

"Hi, Beau."

He looked surprised to see her. "Summer! I see you've met Carly and James."

She nodded.

"I hope you're telling them that I'm a great property manager?"

She laughed. "I wasn't, but you are." She looked at Carly. "Is that important to you?"

"It might be," Carly replied. "If James gets his way. I want to buy a vacation home that's just for us. My husband is interested in renting it out when we're not here."

"Ah." Summer was with Carly on that one. She would hate the idea of people staying in her home when she wasn't there. She smiled at Beau. "Well, if you do end up renting it out, I can certainly vouch for Beau as a property manager."

Beau smiled. "Thank you. I may ask you to make that a written recommendation before you leave."

Ruby looked up at Summer with big sad eyes. "You're leaving? I don't want you to leave! This is my favorite place in the whole wide world, and that's because you're here!"

Summer touched the little girl's shoulder. "I'm not leaving just yet. I'm sure I'll be here longer than you are."

Beau looked at Carly and James and jerked his head toward his truck. "Do you guys want to get going?"

"Noooo!" wailed Ruby. "I want to stay here with Summer Breese!"

Beau ran a hand through his hair and gave Summer an exasperated look. "But don't you want to come see some nice houses?" he asked Ruby.

Ruby made a face at him. "No!"

Summer had to feel sorry for him. He obviously wasn't used to dealing with kids and Ruby appeared headstrong to say the least. "I'm sure you'll have fun with Beau. He's my friend."

Ruby eyed him suspiciously. "You are?"

Beau nodded.

"What's your favorite song then?"

Beau stared at the kid nonplussed.

She scowled. "If Summer Breese is your friend you must like her songs, which one is your favorite?"

"Ruby! Don't be rude," said James. He shot Beau an apologetic look. "Come on. Mr. Remington is going to show us some houses." He took hold of Ruby's hand but she pulled away from him and ran to Summer, wrapping her arms around Summer's legs.

"I don't want to!" she cried.

Summer crouched down beside her. "It's okay, Ruby. I have to leave soon anyway. You can't stay with me. But you can go with my friend, Beau." She grinned up at him. "He really is my friend. He knows all my songs, he just doesn't want to upset me by only picking one as his favorite."

Ruby's lips were pressed into a tight little line, her brows knit together as she looked at Summer. "He's really your friend?"

Summer nodded.

She looked up at Beau and her face relaxed. She cupped her hand over Summer's ear and whispered. "He's very handsome!"

Summer chuckled to herself and nodded again. "He is! So you go with him and your auntie and uncle, and maybe I'll see you again before you leave."

"Okay." Ruby wrapped both arms around Summer's neck and squeezed her tight. Then she went over to Beau and took hold of his hand.

Beau looked at Summer and then down at Ruby. The poor guy was completely thrown by the looks of him.

"Let's go then!" said Ruby.

Summer had to laugh as she watched the four of them get into Beau's truck. Ruby was quite a character. Beau turned the truck around. He raised his hand and rolled his eyes at Summer before he pulled away.

Summer turned her attention back to Carter and Mason who were almost done completing the obstacle course. She had to wonder what either of them would have been like with Ruby. Beau had done pretty well, considering. She had to wonder, too, why Carter's mood seemed to have changed so rapidly. She didn't think that she'd just imagined the change in him. She thought she knew, but she didn't want to assume. When she'd told Ruby that she didn't exactly live here, it had hit her in the gut as it reminded her that she was supposed to leave in a few months—and that would mean leaving Carter. That was when his smile had disappeared. Was he really as sad as she was at the thought of her going back to Nashville? She didn't want to assume, but she didn't feel that she should ask him either.

His smile was back as he completed the course and rode over to her. "They left you in peace then, finally?" he asked.

"Yeah. They're not so bad. I think Ruby is the one in charge." Carter grinned. "No doubt about it. Beau won't take any crap from her, though."

"I don't know about that. I had to convince her that Beau was my friend before she'd even go with him."

"I can't imagine Beau being bossed around by a five year old!"
Summer laughed. "I don't think he could either. I'm guessing
none of you have any experience with little kids?"
Carter didn't quite meet her gaze as he shook his head.
She had to wonder what that was all about, but she didn't get
chance to wonder too long.
"Carter! Mason!"
Summer looked up at the sound of a woman's voice. It was
Mrs. Remington calling her boys as she strode down from the
big house.
Carter glanced over at his mom and then at Summer. "I don't
know what's coming, but knowing her, it'll be something. I'll
make our excuses and get us out of here as quick as I can,
okay?"
Summer smiled. She was in no hurry to leave.
Mason had dismounted and led his horse over to join them at
the fence as Monique arrived.
"Do you all have plans for dinner?" she asked. "I just got off
the phone with Cassidy and she and Shane are coming." She
grinned at Mason. "I talked to Gina, too. She's heading
straight up to the big house when she gets done in the park."
Mason rolled his eyes at Carter as Monique turned to Summer.
"I'd love it if you would join us?"
Carter shot her an apologetic look.
Summer smiled. "I'd love to." She really would, but she wasn't
sure how Carter felt about it. She wanted to give him an out if
he wanted it. "What about the cats, though?" she asked him.
She knew he'd want to at least check on them.
He shrugged and looked uncomfortable. She didn't know what
that meant. Did he think she meant she didn't want to stay?
She tried again, wanting to make it easy for him to go with

whichever he preferred. "If you like I could go see to them while you get done with the horses and then meet you back here?"

He smiled at that. "If you wouldn't mind?"

She grinned. So maybe he did want her to have dinner with his family. "I don't mind at all."

Monique raised an inquiring eyebrow at her.

"Yes, please. I'd love to come to dinner."

Monique smiled. She was quite beautiful. "Wonderful. I hardly ever have all my boys home for dinner any more. And now I get all their ladies too!"

Mason cocked his head to one side. "Did you ask Beau?"

"Of course!" replied Monique. She sighed. "And Chance, too. So, please help me keep Beau in line if he starts. I don't want any arguments at my dinner table."

"Don't worry, Mom," said Carter. "He won't go there."

Mason nodded. "And we'll sidetrack him if he tries."

Summer had some idea what they were talking about, but it surprised her that they expected Beau to start arguments at a family dinner. He didn't strike her to be that kind of guy at all.

Monique smiled at her. "Don't worry; it's nothing horrible. Just little boy squabbles coming out of grown men."

Summer had to laugh at that.

"How about six thirty? Can you all be up at the house by then?"

Mason nodded. "Sure, we can get done here and finish off the others tomorrow."

Summer checked her watch. It'd take her half an hour to drive up to Carter's place, another half an hour back down, that would leave her with an hour to stop and get a shower. "Sounds good to me," she said.

Monique smiled. "I'd better get to work then."

Mason nodded. "Come on, bro. We can put a couple more through the course before dinner."

Carter looked at Summer. "You sure you're okay to go up there?"

"I am, if you trust me with your keys and your truck?"

He smiled and dug his keys out of his pocket. He handed them over with a smile. He was so damned gorgeous! Summer wanted to take him with her and spend the rest of the night alone with him, at his house, in his bed! Instead she smiled back and planted a kiss on his cheek. "I'll see you back here in a little while."

He nodded. "Call me when you're leaving and I'll wait out on the front porch for you."

Summer smiled as she made her way to his truck. He was so sweet.

She climbed into his truck and had to spend a few minutes adjusting the seat and the mirrors. It was a huge truck, she'd never driven anything quite this big before, but as she headed out of the Remington Ranch driveway and turned onto East River Road to head up toward town, she felt very much at home—in the truck and in the valley.

She allowed herself to daydream as she drove. What would life be like if she stayed here? Would it be just like this? Hanging out with Carter and his family, driving his truck around? Feeling happier and more free than she could remember? She sighed. She had a feeling that it would. She loved the idea. But was she brave enough to make the idea a reality? If she was, she needed to separate the desire to stay here from the desire to be with Carter. It wouldn't be right, wouldn't be fair to either of them to put so much pressure on. Would she want to stay here, would this life seem so appealing, if it wasn't about him? She knew the answer, but she didn't know what to do with it.

It took just over half an hour to reach his place. She pulled into the driveway and drove past the nursery. She was surprised to see a car in the driveway. She cut the ignition and peered through the windshield before she got out. She was surprised to see a woman get out of the car and come toward the truck with a big smile on her face. Of course, Summer realized, the smile wasn't for her. Whoever this woman was, she'd be expecting Carter to get out of his truck—not her!

She opened the door and slid down, realizing quite how far down it was when her feet eventually touched the ground and a jarring pain shot up through her ankle.

"Carter! You haven't been in the gym since...oh! Hello."

Summer sucked in a deep breath as the pain shot up her leg.

"Hi!" She managed to gasp at the woman who looked shocked.

"Summer Breese!"

Ugh! This was all she needed. She tried to fake a smile, but it felt more like a grimace. "That's right. And you are?" Even as she said it, she could hear that she sounded less than friendly. She didn't mean to, but damn if her ankle didn't hurt!

The woman frowned. She was pretty, with shoulder length brown hair. She had a great figure. Summer was pretty sure that she must have earned it in the gym. An unpleasant thought struck her—maybe this was the woman who was interested in Carter? She must be.

"Sorry," the woman smiled. "I didn't mean to be rude. I was just surprised. I expected you to be Carter. I'm Melanie."

Summer nodded. She was shocked by the surge of adrenaline flowing through her veins. In a matter of seconds, she'd convinced herself that this *Melanie*, was Carter's friend from the gym—the reason he hadn't wanted to take Summer to the gym with him. She was shocked at the pangs of jealousy that felt worse than the pain in her ankle. Just what was Melanie doing here? She had to wonder. She held her gaze, not knowing what to say. She was feeling all territorial, but knew she had no right to.

"I just stopped by on the off chance he was home."

Summer started to feel a little guilty. Melanie looked embarrassed.

"He's down at the ranch. He's been helping Mason with the horses."

"Oh, I see. I'll get going then. I just… I just wanted a word with him."

Summer smiled now. "Do you want me to ask him to call you?"

"Oh, no! No. It wasn't anything important." Melanie smiled back at her. "It's okay."

Summer felt as though those last two words meant a whole lot. She felt that Melanie was telling her she understood. Carter was with Summer and Melanie was backing off. "Well, it was nice to meet you."

Melanie nodded and gave her a sad smile. "You too. Welcome to the valley. We're not all bad, you know."

"Thank you." Summer didn't know what else to say. She felt as though she'd met a rival and made a friend.

Melanie got back in her car. She gave Summer a little wave as she drove away.

Summer stood there staring after her for a few moments. She wasn't really sure what had just happened. She shook her head and checked her watch. She was sure what did need to happen though. She needed to check on Hero and her kittens, and then she needed to get back down the valley.

Chapter Eleven

Carter dried himself down after his shower. He may not have lived here for years, but he still had his room, just like his brothers. It came in handy on occasions like this. He threw the towel on the bed, and went to the dresser. He still kept clothes here for the times when he stayed over. When he was dressed he ran downstairs and went to help in the kitchen. It was crowded in there. Cassidy was helping his mom. Mason was sitting at the table talking to their dad who was washing his hands in the big farmhouse sink.

"What can I do?" he asked his mom.

She came over to him and cupped his face between her hands. "You can go sit on the porch and wait for that sweet little lady of yours to come back."

He smiled at her. "Don't get carried away, Mom!"

His dad turned and raised an eyebrow at him. "Why not?"

Carter shrugged. "Because, well, just because. Okay?"

His dad gave him a long, hard look. "Come on, son. It's hard *not* to get carried away. This is the first time you've brought a woman to dinner here since…" He stopped.

"It's okay, Dad. You can say it. Since Trisha. And you're right. It is a big deal. Unfortunately for me, though, it's not *that* big of a deal. Summer's awesome. I'm not going to try to fool anyone and pretend that I'm not bowled over, but it's not going to last."

"You don't know that!" cried his mom.

Carter smiled and put a hand on her shoulder. "I do, though. She's only here for a couple of months. We've talked about it. We're being realistic about it. We're going to enjoy the time that we have, but we both know it's all we'll ever have. I'm okay with it." He squeezed his mom's shoulder gently. "I need for you to be okay with it, too."

She looked as though she was about to argue with him again, but he shook his head. "I know you love me and you just want to see me happy. So do this for me? Don't hold out for something that I know isn't going to happen. Just let me enjoy it for what it is." He smiled. "And help me pick up the pieces when she leaves?"

"Oh, Carter." His mom wrapped him in a hug.

He gave Mason a rueful grin over her shoulder.

Cassidy surprised him. "Are you absolutely sure that she's going back to Nashville?"

He straightened up and met her gaze. "What else would she do?"

Cassidy shrugged. "I don't know. I just wondered. You know, with her voice and everything?"

Carter wouldn't allow his mind to venture near the possibility of Summer not leaving. He had to be realistic. "I think her voice is going to be just fine. She seems to be doing better every day; haven't you noticed?"

Cassidy nodded. "Yeah, I suppose so." Carter could tell she had more to say, but he was grateful that she didn't push it.

"So, why don't you go sit out front to wait for her?" asked his mom.

He looked around the kitchen; it didn't look like there was much he could do to help.

Sitting on the big old swing on the porch, he stared out at the mountains. He really couldn't allow himself to think about it. He had to keep his mind closed down to the fact that Summer would be here for just a short time and then she'd be gone. If he accepted that from the start, it should make it easier to deal with the end when it came. Shouldn't it? He shook his head. He wasn't fooling himself, but all he could do was keep on trying to.

He got to his feet when he saw his truck turn into the driveway. It was odd to see his own vehicle approaching the house when he was already here. He smiled at the sight of Summer sitting up high, she must have raised the seat as far as it would go—her nose was almost pressed against the windshield. She looked so damned cute. She was such a little lady. She should look out of place in a big dirty truck, but it suited her. At least in Carter's mind it did.

He ran down the front steps and opened the door for her when she brought the truck to a stop.

"Hi."

"Hey, little lady."

She grinned at that.

"How did you do?"

She nodded. "Momma and the babies are doing fine. I think you might have some permanent house guests there."

Carter had to agree. He'd expected Hero to take her babies and leave just as soon as she could, but she seemed to be settling in and making herself right at home. He'd set out the litter box he'd bought when Buster had first showed up. Hero had been using it as though it was natural to her. He wouldn't mind a bit if she and her kittens wanted to stay. He smiled. "Thanks for going to check on them." He allowed his eyes to wander over her. She must have gone home on the way back to shower and change. She looked gorgeous in a pink shirt and faded blue jeans. Her hair was tied up in a ponytail. He breathed in, inhaling the scent of her. He didn't know what she smelled of, just that it was sweet and he wanted to keep breathing it. He closed his arms around her and she looped hers up around his neck. Her eyes were wide as she leaned into him.

"We don't have to stay too long," he murmured.

She reached up to kiss his lips, her eyes even wider. "Good."

"Come on, guys!" called Shane from the front door.

Carter sighed and reluctantly let go of her. He loved his family, but right now he'd rather bundle Summer into his truck and take her home than go and have dinner with them. He took hold of her hand. She squeezed his as he led her into the house.

~ ~ ~

Summer looked around at all the faces sitting at the huge table. As much as she'd thought she wanted to skip dinner, she was thoroughly enjoying this. The Remingtons obviously cared about each other very much. Their dad, Dave, was a handsome man. It was easy to tell that the brothers had learned how to treat women from their dad's example. He and Monique were openly loving with each other. Summer had to wonder what it must be like to have a love like that; a love that had endured over the years—that had flourished even, all while raising four boys and running a ranch in this beautiful, but harsh corner of the country. The boys all teased and joked with each other—well, all of them except Chance and Beau. Gina seemed to be one of the family and teased along with the rest of them. From what Summer understood, Gina had grown up with the boys and Shane had been her best friend their whole lives. Cassidy was fitting in as though she'd been here her whole life, too. Although that hardly surprised Summer. Cassidy was like that wherever she went.

Dave turned toward her with a smile. "How are you liking the valley so far? It must be very different from what you're used to."

She nodded. "It is. I absolutely love it here." She smiled at Carter. "It's such a beautiful place and such a different pace of life."

"How long do you think you'll be here for?" asked Monique.

She looked at Carter again. "Well, I have three months to rest my voice before I go to see the doctors again."

"And what will you do if your voice isn't better?"

Dave smiled at Summer. "I don't expect you know the answer to that yourself yet, do you?"

Summer shrugged and gave him an apologetic smile. She didn't. And she wasn't about to tell anyone that she didn't even know what she wanted to do if her voice *did* get better either. She turned back to Monique. "Honestly, I'm trying not to think about it too much, yet."

Monique nodded. Summer would love to know what she was really thinking behind her kind smile. She certainly looked as though she had more questions. The trouble was Summer didn't know the answers—yet.

"I don't blame you," said Chance. "I'd have thought that's part of the beauty of being here—that you don't have to think about it all. You don't have to make any decisions. You can just rest and relax and enjoy yourself."

"That's the idea," said Summer. She didn't really know Chance that well. She'd only met him briefly at Cassidy's dinner party, but she liked him. He didn't say too much, but when he did you realized that nothing got by him.

"And how did you enjoy today?" asked Beau. "Did these guys let you ride, or did you just have to watch all day?"

She laughed. "I had a great time watching."

"And we are going to ride," said Carter. "It's just that I was helping Mason today." He shot Summer an apologetic look.

She gave him a reassuring smile. She hoped he knew that she really had enjoyed watching him put the horses through their paces.

"Well," said Gina. "I'm free tomorrow now, so I can help Mason with the rest of the McLellan horses." She looked at Carter. "You two could ride out if you like." She turned to Summer. "You could take my horse, if you want. She'll look after you."

Summer looked at Carter. She didn't want to back him into taking her out riding if he didn't want to.

He smiled. "Thanks, G. But if Summer wants to go, I thought she could ride Lola."

"So did I," said Mason with a smile.

Summer raised an eyebrow at him, remembering that he'd mentioned Lola when they first went out to the barn.

Mason winked at her. "You stick around here long enough, you'll realize that we like to find our perfect partner in a horse. From the first time I met you, I thought you and Lola would be a good match."

Beau laughed. "I never thought of it like that before, but you're right, Mase."

"When am I ever wrong?"

"So, tell me about each of your perfect horses." said Summer. She could certainly see that Mason's theory held true with Carter and Jake from what she'd seen so far. Jake was a gentle giant with kind eyes.

"Well, you met Carter's partner, Jake, already."

"Yes, and I'm following you so far."

"Okay, so then there's Shane's horse, Cookie."

Cassidy laughed. "He's big, good-looking, full of himself."

Shane gave her a mock hurt look.

"But," she added as she patted Shane's arm. "He's got a heart of gold, he's very good natured and he knows how to take care of you."

Summer smiled at the way Shane nodded as he wrapped an arm around Cassidy's shoulders.

"Then there's Troy," continued Mason.

"Go ahead," said Beau. "I'm interested to hear this."

Mason grinned at him. "As if you didn't already know what I'm going to say. Beau's buddy Troy is a bit of a loner. He likes to go off and do his own thing. When you see them all out grazing, Troy is always off by himself." He grinned at Beau. "He likes to make out he's a badass, but once you get to know him, he's a big softie."

Summer smiled at Beau. He smiled back with a shrug. "All true, I'm afraid."

"And what about your horse?" asked Summer. She didn't want Mason to get away with describing himself through his horse in the way he'd just done with his brothers.

Gina laughed. "I think it's fairer if *I* tell you about Storm."

Summer nodded, knowing this would be good.

Gina grinned at Mason. "Storm can be a bit difficult. He's a handful who can be broody at times. It takes a while to earn his trust. He likes to think he's the boss and tends to keep the others in line."

Summer chuckled as she looked around the table to see the brothers nodding and grinning.

"He can't keep Annie in line, though," Shane added.

Mason laughed. "Hell, no. That stubborn little mare gives him a run for his money."

Summer looked at Gina. "I take it Annie's yours?"

"Yep, she sure is. I prefer the word determined to stubborn, but…" She smiled. "You get the idea."

Summer turned to Chance. "And what about you? What's your horse like?"

Chance shrugged. "I guess I just don't get attached in the same way these guys do."

"Don't believe him for a minute," said Carter. "It's just that Chance gets attached to all of them, but doesn't like to admit it."

Chance smiled as he nodded at her. "But I think all this started because of you and Lola. You see, Lola is a sweetheart. She's a gentle soul. She hasn't been here that long. A Californian family bought one of the McMansions up at Suce Creek. They brought Lola with them and wanted to board her here." He shrugged. "They never came out to see her much. They didn't last long in the valley. It only took one winter to scare them off. When they packed up and left, Lola kicked up a real stink. She wouldn't load into the trailer. Seemed like she didn't want to leave, and none of us wanted to see her go, so we bought her. She's one of us now."

Summer didn't know what to say. She stared at Chance and tried to swallow the lump in her throat.

Monique caught her eye and smiled before asking, "Who's going to clear the dishes so I can serve dessert?"

~ ~ ~

It was late by the time they got back to Summer's place. Carter was tired. It had been a long day, and he hadn't been getting too much sleep lately. He seemed to have been spending most of his nights staring at the ceiling, wondering why he wasn't in bed with Summer.

"Are you coming in?" she asked when he pulled up in front of the house.

He nodded. "I have to."

Her eyes shone in the moonlight as she smiled up at him. "Why's that?"

"I'm a man of my word."

"So you're going to tuck me in then?"

He nodded again. He was. He was starting to doubt his own motives in taking so much time. Yes, he was a gentleman and he would never rush a woman into bed, but this wasn't exactly rushing. Was he really just afraid? Afraid of adding to the hurt he was going to feel when Summer left? Sex meant something to him. It wasn't just a quick physical pleasure; it was a deep emotional connection. Yeah, that probably made him weird, but that was how he saw it. Sleeping with Summer would be laying himself wide open, giving her all of himself so that she could tear him apart when she left. He met her gaze and took a deep breath. She was worth it. He climbed out of the truck. She didn't wait for him to come around to open her door. She jumped down and winced as she hit the ground.

"Are you okay?" He hurried to her.

She bit her lip and nodded. "I'm fine. I forget how far down it is. I did the same thing at your house this afternoon."

He took her arm as she stood on one leg to rub her ankle. "Damn!" she muttered.

Carter smiled to himself. He put an arm around her and bent down to hook his other arm behind her knees. He scooped her up and smiled down at her.

She smiled back and looped her arms around his neck. "I like it!"

"So do I." He really did. She was so small, she hardly seemed to weigh anything. He strode up the steps to the front door.

Summer scrabbled in her huge purse for the key. That amused him. No one he knew locked their doors around here. It just wasn't something you needed to do. Eventually she found the key and unlocked the door.

Once they were inside, Carter hesitated in the hallway.

"Straight to bed?" she asked.

He nodded and walked down the hallway and into her bedroom. He could feel his heart hammering in his chest—and it wasn't from the effort of carrying her! He gently laid her down on the bed and then stood there looking at her. He didn't know what to do next. Part of him wanted to lie down beside her, take her in his arms, and make to love to her. Part of him wanted to pull the covers up over her, tuck her in like he'd promised he would and then hightail it out of here.

She smiled and held her arms up to him. How he could he say no to that?

He sat down on the bed and stroked her hair away from her eyes. He let his fingers run on down her cheek. She was so damned beautiful!

"Stay with me?"

He looked deep into her eyes. Yes, they were filled with lust,
but there was something more than that too. Her next words
confirmed it.

"Carter, you know I want you." She reached up to touch his
cheek. "But if it's still too soon, that's okay. I can wait. But I
want to lie here with you. I want to hold you. I want you to
hold me. I want to go to sleep with your arms around me. And
I want to wake up next you in the morning. Please say you'll
stay?"

How in hell could he say no? He nodded slowly, and began to
unbutton his shirt. He loved the way her eyes followed his
fingers. She watched him undo each button, until his shirt
hung open. She sat up and pushed it off his shoulders. The
feel of her small cool hands on his skin drove him crazy with
need for her. He wanted to get out of his jeans, but thought it
best to keep his hard-on trapped, caged behind his zipper for
now.

He drew in a deep breath as she began to unfasten her own
shirt. He found his eyes following her fingers as they worked
their way down. Once her shirt hung loose, she looked up at
him and he dared to push it off her shoulders. She was perfect.
Her skin looked so delicate. Her white lacy bra encased her
pert little breasts. He covered them with his hands and
watched her eyes close. He circled his thumbs around the hard
little peaks that pressed through the lace. He needed to see, to
touch, to taste.

He reached around and unhooked her bra, then slowly slid the
straps down her arms. When it was gone, he closed his hands
around her waist and let his eyes travel over her. She was
perfect—and she was his! Alarm bells went off in his mind.
She *wasn't* his! He shouldn't... This time though, his body
refused to heed the alarms, refused to be denied what it had
been aching for, for so long. Keeping his hands around her

waist, he pulled her to him. Her naked skin felt so soft against his. The smell of her filled his nostrils and his mind as he covered her mouth with his own and kissed her deeply.

Her arms came up around his neck, and as if on a mission of their own, his hands sought her breasts. She moaned into his mouth, making him even harder as he circled her taut nipple with his thumb. All of his resolve crumbled around him as he crushed her to his chest. He needed to make her his own.

Her hands dropped to his waistband. There was no part of him left that wanted to stop her. He bit her bottom lip as she pushed his jeans and his shorts down over his hips. She rubbed her hips against his and the feel of the rough denim against his most sensitive skin reminded him that he was falling behind. He unfastened her jeans and pushed them down and off. He left her panties alone, knowing that that little scrap of lace was a last line of defense between him and the inevitable. He couldn't resist though. He slid his hand inside. His heart beat even faster when he felt how hot and wet she was. She hadn't been kidding that she wanted him! He began to work her with his fingertips and smiled when she moaned again.

His smile faded when her hand closed around him. God that felt good! Too good! She'd make him come in no time if she kept doing that. He shifted his hips away from her and began to tease her opening with his fingers.

"Carter!" she moaned.

She didn't need to say anything else. He knew what she meant. Knew what she wanted. He slid her panties down and off. He couldn't resist ducking his head to taste her nipples, but that just made her more desperate. She wrapped her legs around his, opening herself up to him as she looked up into his eyes and buried her fingers in his hair.

"Carter, please!"

It was a moment he would relive again and again. Summer Breese lay underneath him, legs spread wide open, so she could press her heat against him, enticing him inside as she begged him to make love to her. In the moment, though, all that mattered was his need to be inside her. He propped himself on his elbows, afraid to crush her as he thrust his hips. He thrust deep and cried her name as she clung to him. For a second he froze, afraid that he'd hurt her. He searched her face and she gave the tiniest nod and began to move under him. He joined her rhythm, moving slowly at first. She felt so good, her velvety wetness closing around him with each thrust of his hips. He picked up the pace, losing himself inside her. She responded, bringing her legs up around his back as she bucked underneath him. The tension was building, carrying him higher and higher. He could feel her getting closer, her muscles beginning to tighten around him, increasing the delicious resistance each time he pounded into her. On his next thrust, she dug her fingernails into his back and screamed his name. That took him over the edge. He straightened his arms and thrust deep and hard. His release tore through him and exploded inside her as they frantically melded together.

Eventually he let his head slump onto her shoulder, though he was still careful to keep his weight off her and on his other elbow. She let her legs slide down at the same time that she closed her arms around his back and held him close.

"You were right," she mumbled eventually.

He lifted his head to look down at her. "About what?"

She smiled. "You were worth the wait."

He smiled and dropped a kiss on her lips. "Good. I'd hate to disappoint."

She squeezed her arms tighter around him. "You couldn't if you tried. I just hope I didn't disappoint you?"

He held her gaze. How could she even think that? "You're amazing, Summer. Even more amazing than I dreamed." The way she smiled told him that she really had doubted. He kissed her lips again and then rolled to the side. "Amazing." She snuggled into his side and rested her head on his chest. It felt so natural, so right, to just lie there with her. They didn't need words. Not after what they'd just shared. He twirled a strand of her hair around his finger as he stared up at the ceiling.

"What are you thinking?"

He smiled to himself, wondering if he should tell her.

"What?" she asked. He could hear the smile in her voice.

"Okay then. I'm thinking that I'm an idiot."

"You are not! Why would you even think that?

He chuckled. "Because tonight I'm staring at the ceiling lying here naked with you after we just made love, and I'm thinking about what an idiot I've been to have wasted so many nights up till now staring at the ceiling by myself while you were lying in the next room."

She chuckled, too. "Hmm, I do see your point. But you're definitely not an idiot. Just promise me one thing?"

"What's that?"

"That we won't waste any more nights staring at the ceiling alone?"

"Promise," he said. He didn't smile though. He didn't smile because she'd just reminded him that they would have precious few nights together and he really couldn't afford to waste any of them.

Chapter Twelve

Summer opened her eyes and smiled. She was still nestled into Carter's side with her head on his chest and her arm across his abs. He was still sleeping. She snuggled in closer. Loving the feel of him. Finally, he was here! He'd made love to her and he'd stayed with her—right here in her bed—and nothing had ever felt so right! She looked up at his handsome face, relaxed as he slept. He was beautiful! That may not be a word she'd normally associate with a man, but he was!

It was almost light, but she was done sleeping, she knew that much. Carter stirred and opened his eyes. He smiled and his arm tightened around her.

"G'mornin', darlin'."

She smiled back. She loved the way he called her that. "Good morning yourself."

"It is! The best morning ever."

She chuckled. "Glad to hear it. Do you have any ideas what you'd like to do with it?"

He rolled onto his side and propped himself up on his elbow to smile down at her. "I reckon I could come up with something."

He put his hand on her shoulder and ran it down her arm sending shivers racing through her. She was glad that now the waiting was over, he seemed keen to make up for lost time. "Oh yeah? And what might that be?" He raised an eyebrow and lay back down on his back. "I thought maybe I could take you for a ride." It was her turn to prop herself up and look down at him. "A ride? You mean out in the mountains? On Lola?" He smiled. "Maybe later." He caught hold of her hand and guided it under the sheet. He was hot and hard and very much awake. "But for now I was thinking more of a ride right here, on this."

His words set her pulse racing. He certainly didn't seem too shy this morning. He closed her fingers around his thick shaft and began to move her hand up and down the length of him. Yes, please! She got up on her hands and knees and made to straddle him, just the thought of what he wanted had her wet and ready.

He surprised her with the speed with which he turned her. Somehow she was on her back and he was smiling down at her. "Hold on a minute, missy. There's no rush. We need to make sure you're all warmed up and ready before we ride."

She smiled. "Oh, I am. More than ready!"

She pushed her hips up against him, wanting to feel his hard shaft pressing into her.

He shook his head slowly and reached his hand down between them. His fingers found their way between her legs and sent tingles of anticipation rushing through her. She thrust her hips again, wanting more than just his fingers.

He shook his head again. "You know I like to take it slow."

Oh, no! He was going to tease her? "But, I thought we were past that?"

He began to circle her clit, making it hard to concentrate on his words. "We are, but now we get to savor every single moment."

Hmm, she didn't exactly want to argue with that! Every single moment of what he was doing right now felt wonderful. She relaxed and gave in to the sensations. He dipped a finger inside her at the same moment that his hot mouth came down on her neck. She began to move her hips in time with his hand. She wanted to feel him inside her. She brought her arms up around his neck and spread her legs wider, hoping that he'd take the hint and give her what she wanted so badly.

Instead he turned again, rolling onto his back and drawing her with him. She straddled him and sat up with a smile. He smiled up at her and rocked his hips.

"Ride me, darlin'."

She wasn't about to argue! She closed her fingers around him and guided him to her entrance. His hand joined hers and he began to stroke her again. He was driving her wild. She let herself slide slowly down onto him, surrendering herself to the rocking of his hips and gentle pressure of his fingertips against her clit. She closed her eyes and let her head fall back. She wasn't going to last long, but she wanted to do as he'd said and savor every moment.

His hands came up and closed around her waist as his rocking changed to thrusting. He held her in place, pulling her down to take him deeper and deeper. It felt as though he was filling her with every thrust. Her breasts bounced as she rode him. She grasped his wrists and hung on tight as he took her on the ride of her life. He met her gaze and smiled as he took her closer and closer to the edge. She felt him tense and. that was all it took to trigger her climax.

"Carter!" she screamed as he came with her. He held her still and continued to thrust deep and hard. She felt as though she'd lost control of her own body. Carter now controlled every cell of her being, and he demanded that every cell dissolve in exquisite pleasure. Wave after wave crashed through her, taking her soaring away. Her muscles clung to him as if he were the only solid point in a melting universe. When he finally lay still, she lay down on his chest breathing hard. She'd never come like that in her life! His hands came up to tangle in her hair and he nuzzled his lips into her neck.

"You're a good rider."

"Not yet, but if you give me lots of lessons I think I could learn."

"Lots of lessons?" he asked with a chuckle.

She nodded. "Lots and lots and lots. It might take me a lifetime to perfect it, but we can have fun trying."

He didn't chuckle at that. In fact, he lay quite still. Oh, crap! Why had she said anything about a lifetime? The one big dark cloud hanging over their heads was the fact that they would only have a short time together, and she'd had to go and talk about a lifetime? Especially at a moment like this!

She lifted herself to look into his eyes, but he avoided her gaze. Damn! "Carter. I'm sorry."

He pursed his lips. He looked so sad for a moment. Then it was gone. He smiled that smile that melted her heart every time she saw it. "No, I'm sorry. I'm just a big ol' dumbass who got carried away for a minute." He stroked her hair. "I really am sorry. What do you say we get up? Get cleaned up and go do something fun with the day?"

Summer wanted to talk to him, wanted to tell him that she was sorry for mentioning the lifetime when she didn't know if it was possible. She wanted to tell him that a lifetime with him sounded wonderful to her right now. But she knew better. There was no point having a conversation about something that might not be possible, even if they did both decide they wanted it. She rolled off him and stared up at the ceiling for a moment. "Okay. Let's go get a shower."

~ ~ ~

Carter felt a little uncomfortable about not helping Mason with the McLellan horses. He didn't tell someone he'd do something then not follow through. That wasn't him. When he and Summer arrived at the ranch, he felt a little better about it, though. Gina was out in the arena on one of the mares and she and Mason were joking around. Maybe it was a good thing for the two of them to get some time together.

Summer smiled up at him as they walked toward the barn. "Does that make you feel a little better?" she asked. "You can still go help out if you'd rather do that. I don't mind watching."

He put an arm around her shoulders. He was grateful that she understood, and he knew she really meant it. He shook his head. "I do feel better seeing Mason and G together like that. I don't feel guilty anymore. I can go have fun with you, knowing that Mason's getting done what he needs and having fun with his lady…" He stopped himself short. He didn't want Summer to think that he saw her as his lady in the same way Gina was Mason's. That was different, they were getting married. It wasn't the same. He looked down at her. No matter how much he wished it could be.

She smiled. "Okay then. I'm glad, because I'm looking forward to this."

He raised an eyebrow and gave her a knowing smile. "I know. You proved this morning just how much you like me taking you for a ride."

She pushed at his arm. "I guess I did, didn't I?"

"And I seem to remember you saying something about wanting me to take you for a ride in the mountains?"

Her eyes widened. "Oooh! I could be persuaded."

Carter laughed. He'd only been joking, but he could be persuaded, too.

As they reached the barn, Shane and Cassidy came out laughing together. "Hey, guys! How's it going?" asked Shane.

Carter nodded. "Going great. Is everything okay? What are you doing out here? I thought you took Sundays off?"

Shane laughed. "I do. But Cassidy wanted to ride out. We just brought Cookie and Lady back. We're headed over to see Chance. You know he's going to California this week?"

"That's right. It's his sister's wedding, isn't it?"

Cassidy nodded. "Yeah. We're going to see if he wants to come for lunch at the Riverside, and maybe see if he'll come out one night before he leaves. He's going to miss our engagement bash, but we can hardly compete with his sister's wedding. Do you two want to come along if we can get him out?" She looked at Summer. Carter knew she was checking with her friend whether she wanted to risk being seen out with him.

He relaxed when Summer nodded. "We'd love to." She looked up at him to check. His grin answered for him, even though it was mostly caused by the fact that she'd referred to them as a *we*!

"Okay." Cassidy smiled at Carter. She seemed to understand his reaction and felt the same way. "I'll give you a call when we figure out what's going on."

Shane winked at him. "See you soon, then. Have fun, kiddies. And don't do anything I wouldn't."

"I guess that means we can get up to all kinds of mischief then, little bro."

Shane shrugged. "I guess it does." He grinned at Summer, "Just don't go blaming me if he gets up to anything too wild."

Summer smiled up at Carter. "Don't worry; whatever he gets up to, it's all on him."

Carter smiled back as he led her into the barn. He was glad that she saw him as his own man, responsible for his own actions and decisions. Sometimes he felt like a pale reflection compared to the larger-than-life Shane.

He stopped when he reached Lola's stall. "So, it's time for the two of you to get to know each other."

Summer reached up to rub the mare's nose. "I feel as though we already do. She feels like an old friend."

Carter nodded. He couldn't help thinking back to the conversation at dinner last night. He would love for Lola to become Summer's horse. He would love for their stories to mirror each other. He sucked in a deep breath. That would mean Summer finding that life here in the valley suited her better than the life she'd left behind. He had to be realistic. Lola's former owners might have turned their back on her, but he could hardly see Summer's people—her sister, her record label, hell, even her fans—giving her up so easily. Even if she did want to stay.

"Are you okay?"

He nodded. "I'm just fine." He smiled and dropped a kiss on her lips. "Come on. Let's bring her out and we'll get her and Jake saddled up."

~ ~ ~

Summer smiled to herself as the horses picked their way up the trail. She was enjoying this. She hadn't ridden for years, but she'd felt right at home as soon as she was in the saddle. Lola had everything to do with that. She'd turned her head to look up at Summer, as if to check that she was okay. Summer knew that they'd become great friends. It might have been a long time since she'd been around horses, but one thing that had stuck with her was that what mattered most was the trust between horse and rider. She trusted Lola to take care of her, and she hoped that Lola trusted her not to interfere or mess up.

They were making their way single file up a rocky path. They'd climbed so far that it was cooler up here. Summer was grateful for her jacket. She'd been about to leave it behind, but Carter had suggested she bring it along.

He turned in his saddle and smiled at her. "How are you holding up?"

"This is wonderful! Thank you. Lola is awesome." She reached her arm out over the view of the valley below them. "And it's so beautiful. I mean this place is gorgeous no matter where you are, but seeing it from up here, it's spectacular!" It really was. The valley was maybe fifty miles long and twenty miles wide. From this point they could see almost all of it. The snowcapped peaks seemed to sparkle in the sun, shining stark white against a deep blue sky.

Carter nodded. He seemed to take pride in the place, as though she were paying him a personal compliment by admiring the place. "It is beautiful, isn't it?"

"It's gorgeous." Seeing the way he reacted, the way he obviously loved the place so much, Summer knew for absolute certain there was no way he'd ever leave. This place was more than just where he lived; it was a part of who he was. The tiny part of her that had been wondering whether they might continue seeing each other when she had to leave saw the truth in that moment. If she wanted Carter, she had to want a life here. She pursed her lips. She thought she did, but was that realistic?

He reined Jake in and waited for her to bring Lola alongside. "Are you okay?"

She nodded.

"What is it though? For a moment there you looked so sad." She met his gaze for a moment. "It's nothing." She didn't know what to say. There was no point in trying to explain it to him. She wanted to enjoy their time together, not spoil it with sad talk about what might never be.

His big brown eyes were full of questions. It seemed as though he found his answers and he nodded. If he did understand what she was thinking, he apparently didn't want to go there either. He patted the pack behind him. "Let's keep going, there's a great picnic spot a little farther up. If you like the view from here, you'll love it up there."

"Sounds perfect." She urged Lola forward and smiled a bright smile, determined to enjoy the day. She'd be crazy not to. No matter what the future might or might not hold, today she was with this beautiful man, in this beautiful place—how could she *not* enjoy that?

Chapter Thirteen

Carter was tired when he got home from work on Monday afternoon. It'd been a great few days, but he hadn't gotten much sleep. He smiled as he let himself in the back door. He'd never been happier! He peeked into the laundry room where Hero was nursing her kittens. She looked up and blinked at him happily. He was starting to think that Summer was right and he had four new permanent house guests. He couldn't help but wish that Summer herself would become a permanent feature in his life. He'd loved spending the weekend with her. He'd only left her place this morning and only then because he was starting a new job today. He'd gotten the contract to redo and maintain the grounds of the county offices up in town. He'd needed to be on site for the first day of the job. Things had gone well and his guys had a handle on what he wanted done. He didn't plan to spend all his time there over the next few weeks.

He set out fresh food and water for Hero and then went to check the shed. Buster was lounging on one of the shelves and came to rub around Carter's legs in greeting. He butted Carter's arm as he filled up the food bowl and refreshed the water.

"How's it going, old fella?"

Buster butted his arm again, but didn't seem to have much to say for himself as he buried his face in the bowl.

Carter left him to it. He was headed for the gym. He needed to fit in a quick workout before he went back down to see Summer tonight. He wanted to get back to her place as soon as he could, but four days with no gym had him feeling like crap. He wouldn't stay too long, but he needed to go.

He was almost done with his workout when he spotted Melanie. He sighed and focused on another set of reps. He felt bad that he'd dodged her last week, but he still didn't feel like talking to her. It seemed he wasn't going to have a choice about it tonight, though. She came straight over. At least she waited for him to finish his set before she spoke.

"Hey."

He nodded. "Hi, Melanie." He decided he needed to just go for it. Tell her he wasn't interested and get this over with as soon as possible. "Listen, I'm sorry I didn't get back to you about maybe going out, but…"

She held her hand up with a smile. "That's okay. I get it. I'll admit I was a little disappointed at first, but when I ran into Summer at your place, I understood. You could have just told me, you know."

Carter frowned. Summer hadn't mentioned running into Melanie, and what was it that he could have just told her. He waited for her to explain.

She looked around before she spoke again, as if to check that no one was listening. "You could have told me that you two were seeing each other."

Had Summer told her that they were? "We weren't when you and I talked."

Melanie smiled. "But you are now! Don't worry, I didn't come to give you a hard time. I just wanted to let you know I'm happy for you." She seemed to mean it.

He shrugged. "Thanks." He didn't know what else to say. Neither did Melanie. "Well, I guess I'll see you around."

"Yeah. See ya."

~ ~ ~

Summer sat out on the deck. She'd had a lovely peaceful day. She'd spent most of it counting down the hours until Carter would return, but other than that she hadn't done much at all. Now she sat looking out at the river. Hopefully he'd be here before too long. He'd said he was going to hit the gym first. Summer had wondered whether she should tell him about Melanie. She'd completely forgotten about it on Friday. There didn't seem much point now though. He'd see her himself. She had to wonder what the history was between the two of them, but had to admit it was none of her business.

She did a double take when she saw movement on the path down by the river. She leaned forward and peered down there, then laughed when she realized it was Cassidy.

"Hola, chica!" she called and waved up at Summer.

"Hi! What on earth are you doing down there?"

Cassidy laughed. "I'm practicing braving the wild!"

"Huh?"

"Hang on. I'm coming up. I'll tell you when I get there."

Summer watched as she climbed the steps to the deck and then flopped down in the chair beside her.

"Are you going to offer me a drink?"

Summer grinned. "Let me guess—vino?"

"Yes, please!"

Summer went inside and returned with two glasses of wine. She handed one to Cassidy before taking her seat again.

Cassidy took a sip then smiled. "Ah, sustenance. It's scary out there you know!"

Summer laughed. "Out where? Where have you been and what are you up to?"

"Like I said, I'm practicing braving the wilderness. You'll come up against it yourself at some point, if Carter ever leaves your side."

"Come up against what?"

"The fact that we live in bear and wolf and who knows what else country. It's all fine and dandy and great to talk about, but what happens when you just want to go for a walk? Do you know where the bears are? Do you know what might leap out and want to eat you?"

Summer laughed. "No, of course I don't." She frowned. "And I suppose you're right. I will come up against it at some point. I'm still just finding my feet here, but what do I do when I want to go hiking?"

"Exactly! I was ashamed to admit it, but I'd been hanging out in my house like it was a little oasis, but I don't want to do that. I want to go out and explore. I don't want to be ridiculously naïve about it, but I certainly don't want to become something's lunch either. I've been asking Shane all kinds of dumb questions, and today I thought it was time to venture out by myself. That little path down by the river from my house to yours seems like just a romantic little walk when you've got a big strong Montana man by your side. It looks a whole lot different when you're by yourself and there's a hungry critter lurking around every corner!"

Summer had to laugh. "But you braved it anyway, just to come see me?"

"Nah." Cassidy grinned at her over the rim of her glass. "I came to see you because I was out braving it and needed a drink before I turn around to go back!"

"Thanks! Glad to know I come in handy for something." Summer stuck her tongue out at her friend.

"You're welcome. And while I'm here, how are you doing? It's so different this time. I mean, last time you were here we spent so much time together, but now Shane's at my place and you seem to be spending every waking moment with Carter."

It was true. The two of them had hardly had any time together.

"I'm doing great." She smiled. "I'm loving spending time with Carter, and I know you and Shane are all wrapped up in each other."

"We are, but I want to see you, too. If you can fit me in."

"You know I can. Did you fix anything up with Chance for this week?"

Cassidy shook her head sadly. "He left for California yesterday. His dad had a stroke."

"Oh, no! Is he going to be okay?"

Cassidy shrugged. "I don't know yet. We haven't heard anything. I want to call him, but Shane says he'll call us if he wants to."

"Poor guy. And it must be awful for his sister, just before her wedding."

Cassidy nodded. "There's nothing we can do for them though. And since we're not going to get a night out with everyone, I thought you and I might have a day out."

"What do you want to do?"

"I thought maybe we could go over to Bozeman one day. Have a girly shopping trip?"

"That sounds great, when?"

Cassidy laughed. "Don't worry, we can do it on a weekday when Carter would be at work anyway."

"Thanks." Summer really did want to spend time with Cassidy, but she was glad she wouldn't have to give up a day with Carter in order to do so. She shook her head. That wasn't like her.

"What?" asked Cassidy. "What's bugging you?"

"Just that, I'm not that girl, you know? The girl who skips out on her friends when there's a new man on the scene. I've never been like that. It's just that I keep thinking I want to spend as much time with him as I can. If we're only going to have a short time together, I want to make the most of it."

Cassidy raised an eyebrow and gave her a stern look. "And have you done any more thinking about whether you are going to have just a short time with him?"

Summer shook her head. "I don't know what to think. I don't know what I feel."

Instead of the sympathy she'd been hoping for from her friend, she just got another stern look. "Well, I think you need to figure out how you feel sooner rather than later. And not just for your own sake. It's hard watching Carter fall hook, line, and sinker for you. He's going to be devastated when you leave."

Summer hung her head. "And you think I'm not?"

Cassidy patted her arm gently. "No, I think you're going to be just as bad as he is. What I really think is that you should get your act together and admit right now that you don't want to leave."

Summer's head jerked up. It was true, but she didn't want to admit it even to herself yet. It raised too many questions about how she could stay and would cause too many problems if she did.

Cassidy smiled. "Sorry. I told myself I wasn't going to push, but I hate watching you do this to yourself—and to Carter."

Summer nodded sadly. "Life's not always about what you want though is it? It's about what you have to do."

Cassidy shook her head. "See, you're talking to the wrong girl there. I'd tell you that life is all about what you want to do. The things you *have* to do are just obstacles to be overcome on the way to getting what you want."

"In your world maybe, but it's different for me. What about Autumn? What about Clay? I can't just leave them in the lurch because I want something else."

Cassidy nodded. "No, you can't, and you never would; that's where the obstacle part comes in. You have to find a way not to screw them over, but you can't use them as an excuse to screw yourself over. And that's what you'd be doing you know—screwing yourself over." Cassidy took a long sip of her wine. "Anyways. I talk too much, and it's up to you to figure out what you're going to do and how you're going to get there. It just boils down to, I care about you and I want to see you happy. And I care about Carter, too, and I don't want to see him get hurt."

Summer nodded. "Yeah, thanks. I just wish you were coming up with ways to make it all possible."

"That's for you to do. I can be a pain in your ass, and I can be your cheerleader, but you're the one who has to figure it all out."

Summer took a sip of her own wine and let out a big sigh. "I know."

"Anyways. On to happier subjects. Have you heard from Autumn? Is she coming next weekend?"

"I don't know. She hasn't called me back yet. I'll try her again in the morning."

Cassidy nodded. "You know, when she sees you with Carter, she's going to realize this is big?"

"You think so?" Summer's voice cracked. It had been holding up so well the last few days, but it seemed that stress made it worse.

"We both know so! So you might want to do some thinking about what you want before she gets here."

Summer nodded. Cassidy was right. She might want to just live in the moment and enjoy her time with Carter, but that wasn't going to be fair to anyone around her.

"Sorry," said Cassidy. "I didn't mean to come over and pee on your parade, but I'd hate to see you go into ostrich mode and then have it all blow up in your face when you finally get your head out of the sand."

Summer nodded. "Thanks. I know you're just looking out for me..." She looked up at the sound of a truck coming down the driveway. It was Carter.

"I'm outta here," said Cassidy and downed the rest of her wine in a gulp. "Have a great evening, I'll call you tomorrow about a day out, okay?"

"Okay. You don't need to go, though. Stick around and say hello."

Cassidy shook her head. "Nah. It kills me to see the way he looks at you. If you do leave, I'm going to be helping him to pick up the pieces, you know?"

Summer's heart hurt at that. She didn't want to be responsible for making him miserable! She didn't want to think about how miserable she would be either. "Say it like it is, why don't you?"

Cassidy shrugged. "Always have, always will. You know me. I'm not trying to be a bitch, but you know I'll always tell you the truth."

Summer nodded. She did. It was one of things that made Cassidy who she was, and Summer loved her for it. "Okay, well, I guess I'll talk to you tomorrow then."

Cassidy was already on her feet and making her way down the steps. "Yep. Say hi to Carter for me. And keep your fingers crossed I don't run into any hungry wolves on the way home."

"Do you want me to give you a ride?"

Cassidy shook her head with a grin. "I'll be fine. It's the wolves who need to watch out for themselves."

Summer didn't doubt it. "Text me when you get home then."

"Okay, see ya."

Summer watched her make her way down the path back to the river. She turned and grinned before she disappeared around the stand of cottonwood trees. She'd be fine; Summer wasn't worried about her at all.

She turned back to the front of the house as Carter's truck came to a stop and he climbed out. She took a moment to just admire him. He was all kinds of sexy. His hair was still damp from the shower. He wore a black T-shirt with the sleeves rolled up a little. She's always thought that big guys did that to show off their bulging biceps. Carter had reassured her that it was simply because the sleeves weren't big enough; they restricted movement if he left them down. In his case she believed him.

He pulled his bag out of the back of his truck and turned to smile up at her. "Is Cassidy here?"

"She just left."

He looked puzzled.

"She walked."

Carter looked concerned. "Down by the river?"

"Yes."

"She needs to be careful."

Summer laughed. "Don't worry, she knows. She says it's the wolves and bears who need to be afraid."

Carter laughed with her. "She may have a point there."

He ran up the front steps and came to her. She reached her arms up around his neck and stood on tiptoe to kiss him.

"I missed you."

He smiled. "I missed you, too."

"You're here now though, and that's all that counts." Even as she said it, her conversation with Cassidy echoed in her mind. It wasn't really *all* that counted, was it? What really counted was what the future would hold. And no matter what it held, she didn't want either of them to end up getting hurt.

As Carter closed his arms around her and kissed her back, she leaned into him, wishing that he could be her future. The thought took her by surprise, but it was true. She did! She didn't see how he could be though. Even if that was what he wanted, too.

Chapter Fourteen

By the time weekend rolled around, Carter was more than ready for it. He'd ended up needing to be on site most of the week with his new job. He'd spent Monday and Tuesday nights at Summer's place, but by Wednesday she'd suggested that she come up to see him. He'd gladly agreed. He loved going to see her, but it was adding an extra half hour onto his drive at the beginning and end of every day. Last night they'd stayed here at his place, too, since they were headed to the airport at lunchtime to pick up Summer's sister, Autumn. Carter wasn't sure how he felt about that. Well, he knew he was nervous, but other than that he wasn't sure. Part of him knew he would be under scrutiny. Part of him wanted to defend himself against this woman he'd pictured in his mind; she was almost a wicked stepsister in the version he'd created. Another part of him knew—or at least hoped—that he was being unfair. That Autumn wouldn't have a problem with him.

Summer came down the stairs, she was fresh from the shower and wrapped in a towel. He let his eyes wander over her. He wanted to take her back upstairs and unravel the towel.

She gave him a knowing smile. "You want to?"

He chuckled and shook his head. "You know I want to, but I don't know if I have the strength! You've worn me out this week." It was true. While they might have taken their time before they made love for the first time, they'd certainly been making up for it ever since. Summer may seem sweet and innocent, but she was insatiable in the bedroom.

She smiled. "Sorry, I just can't seem to get enough of you. And since you keep saying you're not going to stay with me tonight…"

"I can't. Autumn's going to be staying with you. It wouldn't be right."

Summer rolled her eyes. "Why not? She knows all about you. Knows that we're seeing each other. It's not as though she's sharing a room with me, just staying at my place."

Carter felt dumb. He shrugged and gave her an apologetic smile. "I know, darlin'. And I'm sorry. It just doesn't seem right to me. I'll drive you both home from the party and then I'll come on home. If she wants to, I'll come take you both out for breakfast in the morning?"

Summer nodded. "Yes, please. We need to get her back to the airport early in the afternoon, so breakfast would be good." She waggled her eyebrows at him. "And after we drop her off we can come back here."

He laughed. "I thought you wanted to ride again tomorrow."

"I do!"

"I meant Lola, not me!"

She chuckled. "Maybe. If there's time."

Sometimes he found it hard to believe just how lucky he was. Summer Breese was standing in his kitchen, wearing just a towel and a smile and she was telling him how much she wanted him. It almost seemed too good to be true. He knew it was true, but what bothered him most was knowing that it was too good to last. He was still wary of her sister—her business manager—who, no doubt, wanted her back in Nashville, and back to her singing as soon as possible. Summer came to him and put a hand on his arm. "What? What changed?"

He met her gaze. There seemed to be so many of these moments; moments when one or the other of them would go quiet as they realized how fragile all of this was. He shook his head. He didn't want to talk about it, didn't want to dampen her spirits or spoil the day. But he didn't want to keep avoiding it either. They both crept around the elephant in the room, but it was still there. "Nothing changed, Summer. It just hit me again."

"What did?"

He sighed. "The fact that we're kidding ourselves. And we're trying to kid each other. We're both trying to enjoy every minute we get, but we both know it's not going anywhere. Sometimes it just hits me. It makes me sad." He touched her cheek and smiled. "But I don't want to be sad right now. There's going to be plenty of time for that when you're gone."

She covered his hand with her own and pressed her cheek into his palm. Her eyes were big and sad. "I know what you mean. It hits me too; we can be laughing and then it sneaks up and steals my breath away. I don't want it to end, Carter…"

His heart hammered in his chest as she searched for her next words.

"…I don't know what we can do."

He shook his head sadly. Neither did he. His life was here. Hers was in Nashville. That was all there was to it. "All we can do is what we've been doing. Enjoy what we have, while we have it."

She nodded. "But I want more. I just. I don't know how."

He wrapped his arms around her and held her close to his chest. He didn't want to let go—ever. But he knew he would have to. She tilted her head back to look up at him. Her eyes shone with tears. That killed him. He never, ever wanted to be the guy who made her cry.

He gently swiped his thumb under her eye. "Don't cry, darlin'." There was a lump in his own throat as he spoke. "You're going to be just fine. You'll go back to your life, you'll go back to your singing. You'll be great. You'll be happy. I'll be just a memory—hopefully one that makes you smile sometimes."

Two big fat tears rolled down her cheeks. "I don't want you to be a memory though!"

He shrugged as he wiped the tears away. Neither did he. But he didn't see any other way.

"Carter, I…"

He hated that she was sobbing now. He held her close to his chest and tried to quiet her. This was killing him. He hadn't taken this into account. He'd felt it was all worth the risk, because he'd only been thinking about the pain that *he* would have to go through when it ended. Seeing her like this, he realized that she was going to hurt, too. And that was the last thing in the world he wanted. He felt helpless. He was causing pain for the woman he loved, and he'd never, ever meant to.

He drew in a deep breath. The woman he loved? He closed his eyes. Yup. That was what she was. He didn't know when it had happened, but if he was pushed, he'd probably say it was the moment he first met her. He'd let his big dumb ass fall in love with this beautiful, sweet little lady.

He stroked her hair while her sobs subsided. Eventually he tucked his thumb under her chin and tilted her head back to look up at him. He shook his head sadly. "Don't cry."

She blinked away fresh tears. "I'm sorry."

"There's nothing to be sorry for, Summer. We got into this before we realized what it was going to cost us. *I'm* sorry. I didn't understand that it would hurt you."

She gave him a puzzled look.

"I thought it would only hurt me."

She blew out a sigh. "Well, you're wrong there, mister."

"I can see that now. I can see it, but I don't know what to do about it."

She sniffed and gave him a weak smile. "All we can do is what we were trying to do, I suppose. It's going to hurt, so we may as well do our very best to make the hurt worth it."

He smiled back. She was right. That was all they could do—until he could think of something else.

~ ~ ~

Summer held Carter's hand as they stood at the airport waiting for Autumn to arrive. For all she'd reassured him on the drive over here that he had nothing to worry about, she was a little nervous herself. Autumn had been so angry when she'd seen the story in the paper about Summer and Carter the first time she'd been here. They'd gotten past that, but not until Summer had returned to Nashville and reassured her sister that she wasn't about to give up her career and move to Montana to be with Carter. Now she was considering doing just that, she didn't know what Autumn's reaction would be. It wasn't just about her concern for Summer. It was about Autumn's own career, too. She was Summer's business manager. What would she do if Summer no longer had a business to manage? Summer was pretty sure that there were other artists out there who'd love to work with her sister. Autumn was amazing at what she did, but...she sighed. She wasn't going to solve any of it right now.

Carter squeezed her hand. "Are you all right?"

She nodded. He looked nervous as hell. "I'm fine." She smiled. "And so are you! Whatever thoughts we have going around in our heads right now, we both have to stop it. She's my sister and she loves me. She cares about me, and she wants to see me happy." She smiled up at him. "You make me happy, and she'd have to be blind not to see that."

He smiled back at her. Then turned to look as the doors to the ramp opened. Summer waved and tugged on his hand when she saw her sister.

Autumn spotted them and waved back. She hugged Summer when she reached them, and then turned to Carter.

"Nice to meet you, Carter. Now I understand why my sister was in such a hurry to get back here."

A hint of color touched Carter's cheeks as he held his hand out to Autumn. "It's a pleasure to meet you, too, Autumn. Can I take your bag?"

She handed it over with a smile. "Thanks." She turned to Summer "Is there a restroom around here? I can't bring myself to go on the plane."

Summer nodded and pointed toward the ladies room.

"How about I take the bag and bring the truck around?" asked Carter.

Summer smiled. She wasn't sure if he wanted to give her a minute with her sister or get a minute to himself.

"That'd be great, thanks. We'll see you out front." As he started to turn away, she caught his arm and pulled him back. He looked puzzled until she reached her arms up around his neck and planted a peck on his lips. "We won't be long." She felt bad that his neck turned red again, but not as bad as she would have if she'd just let him walk away to take care of the bags and get the car like some kind of chauffeur.

Autumn raised a perfectly groomed eyebrow at her as he walked away. "Was that for my benefit or his?"

Summer chuckled. Her sister didn't miss a trick. "Honestly? I don't know if it was more for your sake, his sake, or mine! I just wanted it, *need* it to be very clear, to both of you, that he is really important to me."

Autumn's angular features softened as she smiled. "I could see that anyway; you didn't need to embarrass the poor guy."

Summer rolled her eyes. "I keep messing this up."

"Then, I'm guessing it's very important to you indeed."

Summer nodded.

Autumn pushed her way into the bathroom. "Sounds as though we need to talk," she called when she'd closed the door behind her. "What do you think he'll make of Nashville?"

Summer covered her face with both her hands. How to answer that one without getting into the whole can of worms right here? "I don't know yet. And for the moment, I'm more concerned with what *you're* going to think of Montana. Hurry up in there, will you? I want to get going so you can see the valley."

Autumn emerged from the bathroom and eyed Summer while she washed her hands. "I sense tension, sister. What are you not telling me?"

Summer's heart stopped beating for a moment. "What do you mean?"

Autumn gave her a skeptical look. "You know exactly what I mean. Stop stalling for time and tell me what you're so worried about. The big show you made out there, the way you just dodged my question about what he's going to make of Nashville. What are you so uptight about?"

Summer stared at her. "I'm so uptight because I want you to like him. I want you to like him because I love him!"

Autumn laughed. "I already knew that!"

Summer had to take a moment to catch up with herself. "You always were the smart one! I didn't even know it until I just told you."

"Oh, wow! You mean you haven't told him?"

"How could I? I seriously did not know it until right now."

"Well, I wouldn't worry about it. He loves you, too. It took me all of two seconds to realize that when I walked through the doors and laid eyes on the pair of you." She smiled through pursed lips. "Looks like you've got some catching up to do."

Summer nodded, she did, *they* did. But then, so did Autumn. She needed to catch up on the fact that it didn't really matter what Carter might think of Nashville, because no way on earth would he ever move there. Even if he said he would, Summer wouldn't let him. She couldn't ask that of him.

"Why do I get the feeling there's more to this than you're telling me?"

Autumn really *didn't* miss a trick.

Summer sighed. "It's complicated. For now, can we get out of here? I'll tell you all about it when we get to the house. Carter's going to drop us off there and then pick us up tonight to go to Cassidy's party."

"Okay, but don't think you're going to be able to hide it from me. I want to know what's going on with you. I want to see you happy. That's what matters most to me."

Summer hoped that she really meant that, but how could she if Summer making herself happy would cost Autumn her job? She let them out of the restroom and pointed to the doors. "Come on, Carter's waiting."

Autumn linked arms with her as they went. "And by the way? He's gorgeous! Are there any more like him? Cassidy got engaged to his brother, right?"

Summer nodded. "She did, but Shane's a different character altogether."

Autumn laughed, "Let me guess there isn't another one like Carter anywhere in the world, let alone amongst his brothers. He's unique—and you got him!"

"That about sums it up." It was true. The part that bothered Summer was whether or not she might get to keep him.

When they reached the house, Autumn had the same reaction as Summer had the first time she'd seen it. She loved it. "It's gorgeous," she said when she'd got out of the truck. She turned around in a circle admiring the views of the mountains in every direction. "I can see why you were in a hurry to get back here."

Summer smiled, relieved that her sister could see and understand why she loved the place so much—even without taking Carter into account, this place had captured her heart.

Carter brought Autumn's bag around. "Do you want me to take this in, before I get going?"

"Aren't you going to stay a while?" asked Autumn.

He shook his head. "I need to get going, and besides, I thought the two of you would want some time to catch up with each other. I'll come pick you up tonight for the party."

Summer smiled. "I wish you'd stay, but I know we're not going to be able to persuade you, are we?"

"No. I'll see you later."

She took the bag from his hand and reached up to kiss him. "Okay. Say hi to Hero for me."

He smiled and hugged her to him. When he let go he tipped his hat at Autumn. "You two have yourselves a great afternoon. I'll see you later."

"Bye."

They stood in the driveway in front of the house and watched his truck disappear.

"Wow!" said Autumn.

"What?"

"He's perfect! I mean we need to use him in your next video."

Summer sighed. Carter would never even entertain the idea. She knew it. "Slow down. We don't even know if I'm going to be making any more videos, do we? Remember why I'm here?"

"I do. And I'm starting to wonder. Your voice sounds fine. You're talking just like normal. There must be something in the air—or in your bed—that suits you out here. You sound better already."

Summer chuckled. "There is something in my bed that suits me."

Autumn laughed with her. "You have to tell me, though."

"Tell you what?"

"Well, the size of him, makes me wonder about steroids. And you know what they say about steroids. Did he shrink?"

Summer laughed and shook her head. "He'd never touch steroids, and no, there's nothing small about him!"

"Good to know. On both counts!"

"Come on. Let's get you inside. I want to show you around."

"Okay. Show me around. Give me a glass of wine and tell me everything."

As Summer led her up the steps to the front door, she wondered how much of everything she wanted to tell Autumn.

Chapter Fifteen

Carter sat at the bar with Shane. He smiled to himself as he watched Summer chatting with Cassidy and Autumn. The three of them hadn't stopped talking in what seemed like hours. The party was going great, and after the buffet the three girls had found themselves a table and were catching up. He enjoyed seeing Summer so happy and animated. Her voice seemed to be holding up really well.

Shane slapped him on the back. "You look like a happy man, Big C. I knew you wouldn't have anything to worry about with the sister. She gets it, doesn't she?"

Carter's smile faded a little as he turned to Shane. "I think so. I don't know though. At the end of the day, I'm not really sure that it matters whether she gets it or not."

"Why's that?"

"Because in a couple of months' time, Summer is going to be back in Nashville. None of this will matter anymore, will it?"

Shane frowned. "Why does she have to live in Nashville? There must be plenty of country music singers who don't live there full time."

Carter thought about it. Now he felt really dumb; it had never occurred to him that she didn't have to live there, even if she continued to work there. He shrugged. "It's where her life is."

"It looks to me as though she likes the life she has here better."

Carter sighed. "That's for her to decide, Shane. Not me."

Shane held a hand up. "Sorry, bro."

"That's okay. How about we change the subject, huh?"

A hand came down on his shoulder, making him turn around in a hurry.

"I hope you're not changing the subject because I'm here?" asked Beau. He was joking, but there was a touch of concern in his eyes.

"Course we're not. I'm just tired of talking about the impossible with me and Summer."

"I hope it's not impossible. You two are great together."

Carter rolled his eyes. "Like I was just saying. I'm sick of talking about it."

"Fair enough. Can I ask you one more thing before I drop it?"

"Fire away."

"How likely do you think it is that she might want to buy the house?"

Carter frowned. He had no idea!

Beau punched his arm. "I'm not asking about your future. I'm asking about my investment. Carly and James, the couple you met the other day? They're looking to buy a place. Summer's rental would be perfect for them, but I told her she could have first refusal on it. I don't want to push her—either way. I was just hoping you could give me some idea of what her plans might be."

Carter shook his head. "I wish I could help you, Beau, but I just don't know."

Beau nodded. "Sorry, bro." He shot a look at Shane. "I guess I really am an asshole sometimes, huh?"

Shane grinned at him. "Nah, you're just misunderstood!"

Beau laughed. "Yeah, I am that. I'm not the hard-hearted bastard people make me out to be. Just misunderstood. That's all."

Carter wanted to lighten the mood. "From what I saw the other day, you were a real sweetie pie with that little kid."

Beau rolled his eyes. "Ruby? The kid's a monster!"

Carter laughed. "She's adorable!"

"Yeah, an adorable little monster. She's a two foot tyrant! She scares me shitless!"

Shane laughed. "She's Carly and James's niece, right? She's quite the little character."

"That's a nice way of putting it," said Beau.

"Yeah, I'm not surprised her mom needed a break from her. I don't think Carly and James knew what they were letting themselves in for, bringing her out here on vacation," said Shane.

"From what they told me, her mom has had a lot going lately. Had a rough ride by the sounds of it. If they do buy a place here she might come stay in it for a while."

"Well, back to your original question," said Carter. "I honestly don't know if Summer is interested in buying the place. I hope she is."

Shane grinned at him. "It'd be quite a commute to work for her, but I get the feeling she'd think it was worth it."

Carter nodded. He didn't want to keep thinking about it. It made his head hurt to keep wondering over what might happen. He wanted to get back to just enjoying what they had while they had it.

"Is that her sister with her and Cassidy?" asked Beau.

"Yeah, that's Autumn. She's cool."

Shane nodded. "I like her. I didn't know what to expect, but she is pretty cool."

Carter watched Beau cast an appraising eye over Summer's sister. "You want me to introduce you?"

Beau shook his head. "No, thanks. I wouldn't want to venture into the middle of three women talking up a storm like they are!"

Carter laughed. "Wise man."

~ ~ ~

Summer looked over her shoulder to where Carter was sitting at the bar with his brothers.

"Don't worry," said Autumn. "He isn't going anywhere."

Summer gave her a sheepish grin. "I didn't think he was, I just like to look."

Autumn laughed. "Well, I can understand that. He's a good-looking guy. They both are!" She watched for a minute. "Who's that with them? It's got to be another brother."

"That's Beau, the black sheep," said Cassidy.

Autumn raised an eyebrow, looking interested. "Tell me more. You know I like the bad boys."

"He's not a bad boy," said Summer quickly. "He's a sweetheart really. He's just more reserved than the others."

Cassidy laughed. "Yeah, he's not your kind of bad boy, Autumn. Not your type at all."

"Ah well. He's definitely good to look at. They all are. I just feel better about looking at one that doesn't already belong to one of you!"

Cassidy caught Summer's eye. She shrugged. She knew Cassidy wanted to know if she'd made any decisions, and if she was ready to talk to Autumn about them. She didn't have any answers though.

Autumn looked at her. There wasn't going to be any getting off the hook it seemed.

"So what are you thinking, are you planning on buying the house?"

"Yes!" She hadn't known it until her sister had asked her, but now she seized upon it as one decision that she could make easily. And one that shouldn't have any negative repercussions for anyone.

She looked at them both. "It's a great house, isn't it? I do love it."

"But not nearly as much as you love Carter?" asked Autumn.

Cassidy's eyebrows shot up.

"Don't be offended that she hasn't told you," said Autumn. "She hasn't told him yet, either."

Cassidy held Summer's gaze.

She shrugged. "I didn't realize it myself until madam here arrived."

"And where does it leave you?" asked Cassidy.

Summer shrugged again. "I have no idea."

"I do," said Autumn with a grin. "It'll open up some awesome promo opportunities for you. I'm going to have so much fun with this. I can see it now. Sweet little Summer is back. She's won her battle to recover her voice, and now she has the perfect all American cowboy on her arm as she returns triumphant to Nashville! I was serious you know, Summer. We need to use him in your next video."

Cassidy looked as horrified as Summer felt.

"No! Autumn, that's not going to work. Carter would never go for any of that, and I wouldn't ask him to!"

Autumn smiled. "I bet you he would! He'd do anything for you."

Summer shook her head adamantly. "I wouldn't ask him to. He'd hate it. He'd hate Nashville."

Autumn frowned. "Well, if you two are going to have anything together he's going to have to get used to Nashville, isn't he?"

Summer sighed.

"What are you saying?" Autumn looked worried now.

"I'm not saying anything yet. We don't even know if I'll be able to sing again anyway."

"You're not talking about throwing in the towel are you?"

"No." She wasn't, but only because she didn't want to do that to her sister. She felt like crap. No matter what she did she was going to hurt one of the two people who meant the most in the world to her.

She smiled at Autumn. "I don't know what I'm saying. I don't know what I want. I do know I don't want to hurt Carter and I don't want to mess things up for you. Give me some time? Let me figure out what I want?"

Autumn nodded. "Of course. You know I only want what's best for you."

Summer just wished that what was best for her wouldn't turn out to be what was worst for her sister.

Cassidy looked from Summer to Autumn and back again. "This is all very touching, and I'm sure you'll figure it out, but for now, can we remember that this is supposed to be my engagement party? Let's go find those guys and dance with them, can we?"

Summer smiled. She knew Cassidy wasn't nearly as heartless as she was trying to appear. She just wanted them to move on from a matter that they weren't going to resolve right here and now anyway.

Autumn grinned at her. "It's good to know our Cass hasn't changed. She can't have the spotlight taken away from her for more than a couple of minutes at a time."

"She always was self-centered." Summer stuck her tongue out at her friend.

Cassidy shrugged. "What can I say, I'm special!"

As they made their way over to the bar to join the guys, Summer was grateful to Cassidy. She did have a lot of thinking to do, but what she wanted most right now was to be with Carter. To feel his arms around her as they danced. To forget all the problems the future might hold and just enjoy this evening.

~ ~ ~

Carter smiled when he saw them approaching. Summer came straight to him and he slid down from his stool and put an arm around her shoulders. "Are you okay?"

"I'm great. We came to see if you want to dance?"

Shane laughed. "Carter doesn't dance."

She looked up at him.

"Ignore my little brother. I don't usually dance, but that doesn't mean I can't—or that I don't want to."

He led her out onto the dance floor and closed his arms around her. She rested one hand against his chest and looped the other up around his neck. Hell, if dancing meant he got to hold her like this, he'd dance forever!

"How are you holding up?" he asked as they swayed to the music.

She nodded. "My throat's feeling a bit raspy, but other than that I'm okay."

He smiled. "I'm surprised you've got any voice left at all."

She laughed. "Cassidy and Autumn did most of the talking—honest!"

"Yeah, right. If you say so."

"They did! I just had to answer questions now and again."

He frowned. "What did they want to know?"

She looked the same way she had this morning. Her eyes were sad. "Everything you'd expect. Whether I'm going to buy the house. Whether you're going to come to Nashville. You know, just all those questions that we don't have any answers for."

Carter's heart sank. He did know the answer to one of those questions. He couldn't go to Nashville. He wouldn't survive there. This was his home. And how could he expect her to move here? That was her home.

She touched his cheek and made him look into her eyes.

"What did you tell them?" he asked.

"That I don't know much of anything yet."

He nodded sadly.

She held his gaze. "I told them I don't know much of anything, other than the fact that I love you."

His heart stopped in his chest as he stared down into her eyes. Had he heard that right? He searched her face looking for some clue as to whether she realized what she just said. She was smiling at him hopefully.

"I hope you don't mind me telling them before I told you, but I do love you, Carter."

His heart restarted with a thud. "I love you, Summer. I didn't want to tell you. Didn't want to make any of this harder on you than it already is, but I love you."

Her smile grew bigger, her eyes sparkled and she hugged him tight.

"You know what they say, don't you? They say that love will always find a way."

He nodded, hoping with all his heart that *they* were right.

It was after midnight when he pulled up in front of Summer's house. Carter kept calling it that, but he had to wonder whether it ever really would be hers. Would she buy the place? Make this at least a part-time home?

Autumn leaned forward from the back seat and put a hand on his shoulder. "Please don't tell me that you're going to drive all the way back to your house, just because of me. It'll take you another half hour."

He turned to smile at her. "It's okay."

"It is not, cowboy. I don't like the idea at all. We've seen how many deer lurking in the bushes just on the way back here? I'd be worried to death about you driving all the way home."

"How about I call when I get there?"

She shook her head. "How about you stop arguing and just stay here?"

He really didn't feel like driving home, and she was making it pretty obvious that she didn't have a problem with him staying.

He looked at Summer. She smiled. "I'd stay if I were you. You know I want you to, and arguing with my sister is never a wise move."

"Okay. I give in."

"Good," said Autumn. "Let's get inside and open a bottle of wine then shall we?"

Once they each had a glass, Autumn went to look out the windows. "The sky is just incredible. I feel stupid saying it, but it does seem so much bigger here. I've never seen so many stars."

"Isn't it amazing," said Summer. "We should bundle up and drink this out on the deck."

Carter took a seat and watched the two sisters as they stared up at the sky. He loved that they appreciated the beauty of the place.

Autumn dropped her gaze and looked at him. "I can see why a person would never want to leave here."

He nodded, unsure whether it was an innocent comment or whether she was somehow interrogating him.

Summer laughed. "I'm going to have to leave this place for a minute at least. The cold has gotten to me already. I have to go pee; I'll be right back."

When she'd closed the patio door behind her, Carter looked back at Autumn. "I do love it here."

"And you love my sister, too."

It wasn't a question.

He nodded. "I love her too much to screw anything up for her, if that's what you're worried about."

Her expression was harsh for a moment, then she relaxed. "I think you're taking me the wrong way, Carter. I'm not trying to warn you off her. I'm trying to see a way that you and she can be together and happy."

Relief swept through him. Though it was short lived. Just because Autumn was on their side didn't make the situation any different, or even any easier. Summer's life was in Nashville. His life was here. "Thanks. All I want is for her to be happy."

Autumn nodded. "Me too. Has she said anything about singing while she's been here?"

"Just that she doesn't know if she'll be able to anymore."

"Has she ever once said she wants to?"

Carter thought about it. "No, she hasn't."

Autumn gave him a grim smile. "Thanks."

He cocked his head to one side, not understanding. Had he messed up somehow?

She smiled. "No, seriously. Thank you. It'll all be okay."

Summer stepped back out onto the deck. "What will?"

"Everything," said Autumn. "Everything will be more than okay if I get just one more glass of wine!"

Carter watched her. Her smile was a little too bright. He didn't think it was because of the wine, though. She seemed as though she'd reached a decision about something, but he had no idea what it might be.

Chapter Sixteen

"I wish you could stay longer," said Summer. They were standing at the airport waiting for the pilots to come in to say they were ready to take Autumn home. Carter had said goodbye at the doors and gone to wait in the truck so the sisters could have a few minutes together.

"Me, too," replied Autumn. "I'm mad at myself now. Before I came all I could think about was keeping it to a short visit. Now I wish I'd taken a couple more days."

"Maybe you can come back soon?"

"Maybe." She didn't sound convinced.

"It's not as though you've got that much going on is it?" Summer knew that Autumn had been working on keeping things going, but while she herself was here resting, her sister couldn't be that busy.

Autumn gave her a mysterious smile. "You'd be surprised. You're not the center of my universe you know. I have a few other things I need to get to work on."

Summer wondered what they might be.

"I'm thinking I can help with setting up Matt's tour."

"Oh! That'd keep you busy." Summer was surprised.

Autumn nodded. "Like I said. You're not the center of my universe." She came and gave Summer a hug. "And please will you remember that while you figure out what your next moves are?"

Summer couldn't see her face as she spoke. She pulled back to look her in the eye. "What do you mean?"

Autumn shrugged and pointed to the doors where the pilots were coming in from the ramp. "Looks like my ride is here. I'm sure you'll be able to figure it out. Just do what's right for you, okay? I'm fine."

"But…" Summer needed her to explain what she really meant, but she was already walking away. She turned when she reached the doors and blew a kiss. "Be happy, little sis." Then she was gone.

Summer stared after her. Was she really saying that she'd be okay? That her career wasn't dependent on Summer's own? And if so what would that mean? Was it really time to give up singing? Could she, before she even knew whether she had to? Summer went over to one of the big leather sofas in the waiting area and sat down. She needed to gather her thoughts. Apparently Autumn had just set her free—if she wanted to be. And she didn't know if she wanted to be. Yes, she wanted to be with Carter. Yes, she wanted to live here, but did she really want to end her career without another thought? She shook her head. She didn't need to decide right now. Part of her wanted to run out to the truck and tell Carter she was free and she could stay! But another part of her felt sad and lost. What would she be if she wasn't a singer anymore? She didn't know how to do anything else—wasn't even sure she would want to. She got to her feet. She wanted to talk to Carter about it.

~ ~ ~

Carter watched her make her way back to the truck. She looked sad and lost, but that was hardly surprising, she'd just said good-bye to her sister and the two of them were obviously close. He got out to meet her and wrapped her in a hug when she reached him.

"Are you okay, darlin'?"

She nodded and looked up at him. "I think so."

"You'll see her again soon."

She smiled. "I know."

It seemed as though something else was bothering her. "But what?"

"Let's get going shall we? I'll tell you on the way."

She didn't speak again until they were on the interstate headed east back toward Livingston. "Autumn told me that I'm not the center of her universe and I need to remember that while I figure out what I want to do."

Carter turned to look at her. "And what do you think she meant by that?" He knew what he thought it meant, but he didn't want to jump to conclusions.

Summer shook her head. "I'm as shocked as you are. I think she means that if I want to stay here, give up singing, she'll be fine." She sighed. "But I don't know that she would be. I don't know what she'd do. I don't want to leave her in the lurch, you know?"

Carter did know. Loyalty to siblings was something he understood very well.

"I don't know what to think. I don't know what to do."

"Call her when she gets home, ask her what she's thinking."

Summer nodded. "I'll have to. I can't do anything that would mess her life up."

Carter reached across and put a hand on her knee. She put
hers on top of it and smiled at him. "Do you think you could
stand it if I were to stick around?"

His heart hammered in his chest, he couldn't help the grin that
spread across his face. "Umm. I'd have to think about it, but
yeah, I think I could I stand it."

She laughed. "Well, if you're not sure…"

He squeezed her thigh. "I'm damned sure and you know it. I'd
love you to stay. Do you think, if you did want to keep on
singing, you could even do that from here? Shane mentioned
last night that there are a lot of country singers who don't live
in Nashville. Do you *have* to live there?"

"No. I don't suppose I do. It seems there are all kinds of
options opening up here, aren't there?" She looked stunned,
but happily stunned.

He smiled. "There are. Seems like you might be right. Love
will find a way." He couldn't believe he was saying it. He'd
tried so hard to hold back, he hadn't wanted to put her under
any pressure, but now there really were possibilities opening
up for them.

She leaned across the center console and reached up to kiss his
cheek. "I do love you, Carter."

He grinned and squeezed her knee. "And I love you, darlin'."

~ ~ ~

On Monday morning Autumn pushed her way through the
revolving door at the entrance to McAdam Records. She
clutched her purse to her chest. She had to do this. She'd been
wondering what she was going to do with herself for the next
few months while Summer was up in Montana. Now she was
wondering what she was going to do with the next few years
of her life. She'd loved managing her sister's career, but she'd

always known it wouldn't last forever. Now it seemed as though Summer was ready to begin the next chapter of her life and there was no way Autumn would be the one to hold her back.

She took the elevator up to the third floor and marched into Ashley Devlin's office.

Ashley looked up with a cool smile. "Autumn. What can I do for you?"

"Actually, it's what I can do for you. I heard Matt McConnell's tour needs whipping into shape. I'm here to offer my services."

Ashley pushed her chair back. "That's very generous of you, but shouldn't you be focused on keeping your sister's name out there?"

Autumn smiled. "I can do both." She couldn't afford to mention yet that Summer's ratings may not be an issue for much longer. Summer hadn't made the decision yet, and when she did, it would be for her to choose the timing and make the announcement. Autumn knew she'd have to tread carefully. But the opportunity to manage Matt's tour was one she couldn't let slip through her hands by being too cautious.

Ashley thought it over. "You know it's not my call to make. I think you'd do a great job, but..." she gave Autumn a puzzled look. "It's not like you. Is there anything you want to tell me?"

Autumn sighed, as if she'd been caught out. "Okay, I admit. I don't have enough on my plate while Summer's out of the game. I'm ambitious, I've never made any secret of that. I'd like to extend my reach while my sister's not around."

Ashley nodded and mulled it over.

Autumn knew it was a risk. Ashley saw her as a possible threat to her own position. But she also knew that the label had a lot riding on Matt, and his tour was going to be a big deal for them. The guy he'd brought in with him had proved to be useless *and* an asshole.

"Okay," said Ashley slowly. "I'll put you on Matt's tour." She met Autumn's gaze. "But don't screw up, and don't you dare leave me high and dry when your sister is ready to come back."

"Don't worry, I won't!" She wasn't about to tell Ashley that it was Summer who was likely to leave her high and dry by not coming back!

She smiled to herself as she made her way up to her own office. She needed to get hold of Matt. This tour was going to be great. She was going to make damned sure of it.

As she emerged from the elevator, her cell phone rang— Summer.

~ ~ ~

Summer stared out at the mountains as she waited for her sister to pick up.

"What's up? Are you missing me already? I've not even been gone for twenty-four hours."

Summer laughed. "Hi, yourself. I just needed to talk to you. Ask you what you meant yesterday."

"Come on, Summer. You know full well what I meant. Your heart hasn't been in your singing for a while—even before the problems with your voice started. Your heart *has* found a reason to stay in Montana, though. You've got some big decisions to make, and I need you to make the ones that are right for *you*. I don't want to be a factor. That heart of yours is so big, you'll put my interests before your own if I let you. And I'm not going to let you. If you want to quit, you go ahead and quit, and if you want to come back, you do that, too. But whatever you decide, I want it to be because it's what *you* want. Our careers may have been two sides of the same coin up to this point, but I don't want you thinking of me as a dependent, okay?"

Summer had to laugh. Her sister was many things, but dependent—on anyone or anything—wasn't one of them. "Okay. You made your point."

She could hear Autumn's smile in her voice. "Good, I made myself clear then?"

"Abundantly."

"Okay, well now it's all up to you."

Summer nodded. It was.

Autumn laughed. "It's a tough place to be, isn't it? You have to decide all by yourself. You don't get any easy outs this time."

"I know. It's scary. Normally decisions aren't really decisions, it just a matter of figuring out what options affect whom and picking out the least of all the evils. I'm not used to this."

"I know, little sis, but this is important. This is about your life and what you want it to hold. That shouldn't be based on obligations; it should be based on what you want for yourself. I had to remove myself from the equation so you can focus on you."

"Thanks, Autumn."

"You'd have done the same for me."

Summer nodded. She would.

"Are you still there?"

"Sorry, I am. I'm just wondering. Will you still want to manage me if I decide I do want to come back?"

"Of course I will. I'm not pushing you out into the cold. I'm just trying to get you to a place where you have no external pressures."

"I know. Thanks."

"Well, listen. I have to go. I need to get with Matt and get the ball rolling."

"Okay. Talk soon?"

"Definitely. But for now, go have some fun, rest, relax, take your time."

"I will. Bye."

After she'd hung up Summer let herself out onto the deck and sat down. She liked to sit here and listen to the sounds of the river. It helped her to think. And she had a lot of thinking to do. Autumn had said that she wanted to take the pressure off, but that didn't mean it was all gone. There were different kinds of pressure. Summer still felt a sense of duty to her fans. Was she ready to tell them that the ride was over? And if it was, what would she do from here? Even if she stayed in the valley and she and Carter decided to follow their hearts—wherever that may lead them—what would she do with her life? Hanging out and resting, not doing much other soaking in the hot tub and reading was all well and good while it was a short term thing. It didn't hold much appeal if it were to be her sole purpose in life though. She needed to be doing something, and out here in the valley she had no idea what she might do. It wasn't as though she could paint like Cassidy, or take amazing photos like Gina. She sighed. She supposed she could sing at the resort? They had bands on the weekends. She shook her head. She really did have a lot of thinking to do.

~ ~ ~

Carter looked up at the sound of his name being called. Beau was striding down Main toward where he was working on the grounds of the library.

"Hey, Carter. How's it going?"

He grinned. "It's going great."

Beau raised an eyebrow. "Glad to hear it. Does that mean I need to knock Summer's place off the list of potentials for Carly and James?"

Carter nodded. He didn't exactly know that Summer would want to buy the place, but he had to believe that s he might.

"Does she want it?"

He had to remember that he and Beau were talking at cross purposes. Beau was interested in whether he might sell a house. Carter himself was interested in what his whole future might hold. "You really should talk to her. Not me. I'm going off what I want, and what I see as possible."

Beau nodded. "Sorry. And there I go chasing my own bottom line again. Honestly, though, bro, I don't care if she rents it or buys it or even moves out of it, if she's going to be with you. Seeing you happy is what matters most."

Carter had to smile. "It's a good job no one else can hear you, you really are blowing your reputation as an asshole here, you know."

Beau punched his arm. "Maybe so, but it's worth it to see my little brother happy."

"Thanks. I'm hopeful, but part of me knows I could still just be setting myself up for a fall."

Beau nodded. "I hope you're not, but even if it works out that way, you'll be okay. I know you will. If it doesn't work out for you two, it won't be like before. Will it?"

Carter shook his head. It wouldn't. "What are you doing here, anyway?"

"I'm on my way back to the office." He looked shifty all of a sudden.

"On your way back from where? What have you been up to?"

Beau laughed. "You don't miss a trick do you? You make out you're all clueless, but you don't fool me."

Carter shrugged.

"Okay. I'll tell you. But don't go telling anyone else. You know how Mason and Gina are going to take over the big house after they get married?"

Carter nodded, hoping this wasn't going anywhere bad. Beau had issues with everything to do with the division of the ranch. He hadn't been happy about Mason and Gina getting the big house—and he certainly hadn't been happy about Chance getting the cabin. "Yeah?"

"Well, when they do move into the big house what are Mom and Dad going to do?"

"I guess I hadn't really thought about it. I mean they're going to be in Arizona for the winter and then, I don't know. I figure they'd just stay at the big house when they're back."

Beau looked skeptical. "And how well do you think that would work out for them? Or Mason and Gina?"

"Hmm, not so good, I guess. I really hadn't given it much thought."

"It didn't seem as though anyone else had either. When I tackled Dad about it, he said they might rent a place from me!"

Carter couldn't see that. He couldn't see his parents being here in the valley and not staying on their own land. It wouldn't be right. He frowned.

"Exactly!" said Beau.

"So what have you been working on?"

Beau grinned. He looked pretty damned pleased with himself. "Well, when Mason and Gina move into the big house, that'll leave the cottage empty, right?"

Carter nodded. "You're going rent it to them?"

Beau sighed. "I'm really not that much of an asshole. You think I'd charge our folks rent on a cottage?"

Carter shrugged and gave him a sheepish grin. "I'm slow remember, I'm just trying to catch up."

"I'm going to *give* them the cottage!"

"Wow!"

Beau nodded. "It's right there across the creek behind the barn. They'll still be on their own land. I know dad wants to take a backseat in the future, but I think he'd go nuts if he couldn't be around at all."

Carter had to agree. He smiled at his brother. "You realize everyone's going to know you're not an asshole when you do this, right?"

Beau pursed his lips and shrugged. "I'm sure they'll all think I have some ulterior motive, but what does it matter? It's not about what anyone thinks; it's about Mom and Dad. I thought they'd take the cabin when they moved out of the big house, but they went and gave it to Chance."

"Can I ask you why you still have such a problem with him? It's not as though he's ever done anything to you."

Beau shook his head. "Let's not go there. I didn't mean to get into that one."

"Fair enough." Carter knew better than to push it. "I think it's awesome that you're going to give them the cottage. I think they'll love it."

"You do?" For all his tough exterior, Beau looked like a little kid seeking approval in that moment.

Carter grasped his shoulder. "I do. I'd better get back to work for now though."

Beau looked around. "It's coming on great. You're really going to leave your mark on this town now you're landscaping all the public areas."

Carter smiled. He hadn't thought of it like that before, but now Beau said it, he liked the idea—very much.

"I'll leave you to it." Beau started to walk away. After a few steps he turned back. "Do you and Summer want to come out for dinner with me one night soon?"

Wow! Carter grinned. "We'd love to."

"Great. I'll call you."

As he watched his brother walk away, Carter thought about how many things were changing. Beau had never asked him to come out for dinner before, and he'd never had a woman to go with before either. It seemed as though everything was changing—and for now at least, it seemed as though the changes were for the better.

Chapter Seventeen

Summer checked herself in the mirror. She looked good. She looked healthy despite or perhaps, if she was honest, because of the few pounds she'd gained in the last couple of weeks. Carter came into the bathroom and slid his arms around her waist as he stood behind her. Looking at their reflection she had to admit that they made a beautiful couple. She held his gaze and smiled.

"Are you sure you're okay with this?" she asked.

"I was coming to ask you the same thing. They're all my family—and it's you that's doing the cooking."

"Well, they're my friends, too. And you've helped with everything."

He really had. When he'd told her that Beau had asked if they'd like to go out for dinner with him one night, she'd suggested that they have him over to her house. It had grown from there and tonight all the Remington boys and their ladies were coming.

"I was hardly going to leave you to do everything was I?"

She smiled. He wasn't. He helped out with as much as he could, despite the fact that he worked hard all day while she sat around and did nothing! It was starting to bother her. When being here had felt like a vacation, she hadn't minded spending her days drifting around the house and not doing much of anything. Now that she was starting to think that this might be her life, she needed to find something constructive to do with herself.

She'd brought Hero and the kittens home with her the other day from Carter's place. It seemed silly to her that he was stopping home to check on them when they could be here with her and she could keep an eye on them the whole time. She enjoyed watching them and she couldn't wait until the kittens were a little bigger and wanted to play, but even so, she needed to find something to do with herself. Playing with kittens could hardly be counted as being a productive member of society.

Carter's arms tightened around her waist. "What are you thinking?"

She smiled. "I'm just wondering about what I'm going to do with myself. I need to feel useful, and I don't."

He turned her around to look at him. "I've been thinking about that too."

She laughed. "You don't like your girlfriend being a lazy good for nothing?"

He shook his head. "You know better than that. It's just that I know you need to be doing something. I was wondering…"

"What?"

"Well, You seem to sing to yourself so much…"

It was true, she did love to sing, not just for an audience, but to herself, as she went about the house, when she cooked, in the shower, anywhere and everywhere really. Since her voice had been holding up so well lately, she'd been singing to herself again, even though she knew she wasn't supposed to.

"And you seem to sing your own little songs."

She smiled. "You noticed?"

He nodded. "It's hard to miss. I know all the songs you've ever put out, but I never recognize any of the ones you sing around the house."

She shrugged. "I make them up as I go along."

"I know. You've always written your own songs. Can't you keep doing that?"

She stared at him. "What for?" She wrote her songs in order to perform them. If she wasn't going to be performing anymore, why would she write?

He shrugged. "Maybe it's a dumb idea. I don't know. I just thought that there are songwriters out there. People who don't sing, but they write. You've always done both, but even if you give up singing you don't have to give up writing, do you?"

She thought about it. He was right. She could still write, but then who would sing her songs? Now she thought about it, most of the people she knew did one or the other, but not both. "I could. I suppose. I've just never even considered it before."

"Like I said, it's probably a dumb idea. I just wondered. I thought it might be a way for you to keep doing something you love."

She nodded. "It's a great idea. I need to get my head around it; but yes, I like it."

The way he smiled made her heart swell with love for him. He was such a good man and he cared about her so much.

"I want you to stay here, you know that. But I don't want you staying here to mean that you have to give everything up either."

"Staying here means I get you."

He nodded. "But that's not enough."

She wanted to argue with him. He meant so much to her, but she knew what he meant. He couldn't be her everything. She needed to create a life for herself here if she was going to be truly happy. She hugged him tight and kissed him. "It's enough for now. I'm going to have to find something to do with myself, you're right. But it'll work out. Right now, we'd better finish getting everything ready before the others start showing up."

~ ~ ~

Carter smiled around the table. This was quite something. To have all his family here together, laughing and having fun.

Summer had made a wonderful dinner and Gina had made a delicious cheesecake that she'd brought for dessert. They were all quiet as they ate it.

Cassidy looked up and laughed. "See, G, you have to take it as a compliment that your cheesecake can shut these guys up for this long."

Gina laughed. "Having grown up with them, you learn what will shut up them up and you roll it out now and then just to get some peace."

Carter smiled. "You've been making this for years and years and it's still my favorite."

"Mine, too," said Mason.

Summer smiled at them. "It's so cool that you all grew up here together and are still so close now. I can't imagine spending my whole life in one place like you all have."

"All except Gina," said Mason.

Carter smiled to himself at the look Mason gave his fiancée.

"She had to go out and wander the world for ten years before she came to her senses and came home."

Gina shook her head at him, but didn't argue.

"What about you, though?" Beau asked Summer. "You and Cassidy went to school with each other, right? You might have moved around a lot, but you've been friends since you were kids, haven't you? I don't get how people can keep friendships going when they don't see each other for months."

Summer smiled at Cassidy. "Some friendships are just like that. There have been times when we haven't seen each other for years, but when we get together again, it's like it was yesterday. To me, if someone is a true friend, it doesn't matter how often you see them, or even how often you talk. What matters is that when you do see each other, nothing has changed. You've got news to catch up on, but you're still the same people. You still love each other."

Carter found himself wondering at her words. Would it be like that for the two of them if she were to go back to Nashville? Would they be able to be apart and then come back together as though no time had lapsed in between? He didn't think so. Maybe that was because love was different from friendship— or maybe it was because he and Summer saw things very differently?

He looked up to find Cassidy watching him. She smiled. She always seemed to know what he was thinking. "It's even better when you get to live right next door to each other, though," she said. "I just wish we could get Autumn out here, too."

Carter didn't see that happening.

"What's she doing while you're here?" asked Beau. "As your manager, I'm guessing she doesn't have much to manage with you gone."

Carter turned to Summer. She looked concerned. She'd told him about her conversation with Autumn, but he knew she was still worried about what Autumn would do. She shrugged. "Apparently she's stepped up to manage Matt McConnell's tour."

"Damn!" said Cassidy. "You didn't tell me this. Do you think she needs me to go down there and give her a hand?"

Carter laughed at the look on Shane's face. "It's a good thing I know you love me!" he said to Cassidy. "A guy could get his feelings hurt hearing his fiancée talk like that."

Cassidy laughed. "Your ego is far too robust for me to dent it."

Shane laughed. "I can't argue with that. I'm just glad you finally understand it."

Cassidy rolled her eyes. "I do." She turned back to Summer. "So how did Autumn swing that one? Is Matt with McAdam Records, too? Are they having her manage the other singers while you're gone?"

Summer shook her head. "I'm really not sure how she swung it. She told me that she's fine if I don't want to sing anymore, then all of a sudden she's managing this tour. I don't know if she's glad to be rid of me, or if she just threw herself at the first thing that came along, to prove there's other work she can be doing."

Cassidy smiled. "Well, Matt McConnell's not a bad thing for a girl to throw herself at!"

"Hey!" Shane gave her a hurt look. "I do have some feelings you know."

Cassidy leaned in and pecked his lips. "You know I'm only joking."

He grinned and pulled her to him. "I do. I just wanted the sympathy vote."

Carter chuckled as Cassidy pushed Shane away. "Asshole," she muttered before turning back to Summer. "If anything, I can see Autumn and Matt getting together, can't you?"

Summer smiled. "I don't know. I can never figure my sister out when it comes to guys."

Shane shot a look at Beau. "I can never figure my brother out when it comes to girls either."

Carter had to wonder what he meant. Beau rarely seemed to have a date. But then who was he to talk?

"I don't know," said Mason. "It seems to me, there's a little blonde who's caught his eye lately."

Beau sighed.

"Who's that, then?" asked Carter wondering what he'd missed.

"They're talking about Ruby again," replied Beau. "The kid seems to have taken a shine to me."

"Yeah, it's so damned cute," said Mason with a laugh. "You should have seen her go running to him yesterday when he came out to the barn to pick them up."

"It may look cute to you," said Beau, "but I never know where I'm up to. One minute I'm her favorite person in the world, the next I've managed to piss her off somehow and she hates me!"

Summer smiled at him. "She's quite a handful. Have Carly and James decided what they're going to do yet? You must have shown them a lot of properties."

"I have, but nothing is ever quite right. Honestly, I think this place would have suited them, but I'm thinking you're going to be staying?"

Carter frowned. He wished Beau wouldn't put her under pressure like that. He was relieved when Summer smiled at him before answering Beau.

"Yes, sorry. This one's taken."

He nodded. "I did want to ask you, though. Would you mind if I brought them over to look at the place? Since they haven't found anything that works for them, they're thinking about building. I thought they might get some ideas from this place." Carter wasn't sure he liked the idea of that, but Summer smiled, gracious as ever. "Of course. That'd be fine. I'm sure Ruby would love to meet the kittens, too."

Beau smiled. "Yeah, maybe they'll keep her distracted so I can actually talk to her aunt and uncle."

"What's the story with her parents?" asked Shane.

Beau shrugged. "All I know is that her mom is Carly's sister. It's just her and Ruby. Sounds as though she had a rough time of it. She used to manage a hotel in wine country. She lost her job when one of the big chains bought the place and brought in their own people. She's been working three jobs since then and applying for any hotel management positions she can find."

Shane rubbed his hand over his chin. "Is she looking to move up here, too?"

"Not that I know of, why?"

"Well, with the guest ranch doing so well, and we're going to be expanding, I've been thinking about bringing someone in to manage the lodge."

"Hmm. I can ask them if you like, but I don't know the first thing about her."

Shane shook his head. "It's just an idea. I haven't started looking for anyone yet, but if this woman fits the bill and just falls into my lap…"

Cassidy pushed at him. "She'd better not just fall into your lap!"

He laughed. "It's just a figure of speech, princess."

Carter laughed. The two of them were always like that. He knew they were totally confident in each other and he was happy for them.

Beau looked at his watch. "I hate to be the first to leave, but I'm the only one who needs to get back up to town. I should get going. Thanks for a wonderful dinner, Summer." He looked around at everyone. "And for a great evening, guys. I really enjoyed this."

That made Carter happy. He'd enjoyed this evening, too. He loved that they all seemed to be getting closer again—and that seemed to have a lot to do with the women who were coming into their lives. He wished Beau could find himself a woman. And he wished that Chance was here and would find someone, too. But he wasn't going to hold his breath on that one!

"I love this," said Gina. "How about we do it again next week? You can all come out to the cottage and I'll make dinner?"

The others all nodded their agreement. It was a date.

~ ~ ~

Once they'd gone, Summer snuggled into Carter on the sofa. He wrapped his big arm around her and smiled down at her.

"I really enjoyed this evening," she said. "Did you?"

He nodded. "I did. Thank you. You know how much I love spending time with my brothers. Tonight was great to me. I'm looking forward to doing it again next week, too."

Summer smiled. So was she. "I think we should make it a thing, you know, a tradition. We can all take turns to host and get together every week. I'd love that."

"Do you think you'll stay long enough for it to become a tradition?"

She nodded. "I do. I'd love to think that we'll be doing it for years and years, and down the line, there will be children, too, playing outside while we make dinner."

Carter's eyes widened at that. Oops! She'd never thought to ask him if he wanted kids. She'd just assumed he would. He was so big on family, and he would make an amazing dad. "You don't like that idea?" she asked.

He tightened his arm around her shoulders and drew her closer. "I *love* that idea." He held her gaze. "Especially if you mean *our* kids? I mean, yes, nephews and nieces will be awesome, but our kids? You and me? Is that what you meant?"

She nodded. "I did. I know it's too soon to talk about that, but I just pictured it and had to say it."

His eyes shone happily. "I would love that, Summer. More than you know."

She rested her head against his chest and they sat there in silence for a few minutes. Both lost in their own thoughts.

"If I bought this place, would you move down here with me?" she asked. She'd been wondering about how it all would work and now that they'd talked about kids, she felt a little more confident to ask about where they might live—it didn't occur to her that she might need to ask *if* he wanted to live with her—just *where*.

He nodded. "I could hardly ask you to move into my place, could I?"

"Why not?"

"It's not exactly up to your standard, is it?"

She sat up. "I love your place!"

He chuckled. "You love it while it's mine and it's just a simple guy place. I don't think you'd love it if you had to live there."

He was right, even if she didn't want to admit it. "I like it down here in the valley. You're all the way up in town. I thought you might like to be back down here, closer to your family again."

He smiled at her. "I just want to be close to you, wherever you are."

She smiled back. "Well, where I am right now is on the sofa. Next to you."

He lay back and pulled her with him. "And I want to be close to you."

She looped her arms up around his neck and pressed her body against his. "Like this?"

His eyes shone as he shook his head. "Closer."

She unbuttoned his shirt and ran her hands over his hard chest. "Like this?"

He was unfastening her jeans, pushing them down over her hips. "Closer still."

When their clothes lay in a pile on the floor, she rubbed her hips against his. "This close?"

He nibbled her bottom lip and his hands closed around her breasts making her moan. "Almost." He muttered as he claimed her mouth. She loved the way he kissed her, deep and slow. He explored her with his tongue and while he did he turned her on her back. She clung to him as he spread her legs and positioned himself above her.

He thrust his hips and entered her. "This close," he said.

She smiled and moved her hips in time with his.

He set up a pounding rhythm and she wrapped her legs around him to hold on for dear life. He was so gentle, most of the time. It always took her by surprise when his lovemaking was wild as it was tonight. He took a handful of her hair and pulled her head back so she was looking up into his eyes. She dug her fingernails into his shoulders and spurred him on. He was carrying her away and there was nothing she could do. There was nothing she wanted to do except go with him. He gasped out a ragged breath and she felt him tense in the moment before he found his release. She writhed under him as her own orgasm took her and the pleasure crashed through her.

When they lay still he lifted his head to smile down at her. "I love you, Summer."

She clung to him. "And I love you."

Chapter Eighteen

Summer went to peer out of the window when she heard a car coming up the driveway. Carter was working up in town, so she doubted he'd be back here midmorning. She didn't know who else might be coming by. She wasn't used to having visitors, so she was a little apprehensive. She was relieved to see Cassidy's new blue Tahoe pulling up outside.

She went to open the front door.

"Hey, chica," called Cassidy as she got out.

"Hi, how are you?" Summer's voice cracked as she spoke. It took her by surprise, she'd been doing so well.

Cassidy ran up the front steps to join her. "I'm better than you, by the sounds of it. How long have you been like that?"

"I haven't," croaked Summer. "I was fine until I saw you."

Cassidy laughed. "Great. Are you saying I'm bad for you? I hope not. I've given myself the day off and came to see if you want to go riding with me?"

That took Summer by surprise. She'd have expected Cassidy to want to go shopping in Bozeman rather than riding. She liked the idea, though. "I'd love to."

"Good. I've been practicing riding on Lady. I started out on Cookie, because he's such a sweetheart, but Lady is more my style."

Summer had to smile. After she'd learned the stories of all the brothers' horses, she'd wondered about Lady. Carter had told her that Lady was a good horse, but she needed a strong rider since she had a mind of her own and liked to dominate. She *should* be Cassidy's horse! "Do you think we're ready to go out by ourselves?"

"If we take Cookie and Lola. Shane won't let me take Lady by myself yet." She grinned. "Normally I wouldn't take orders from him, as you well know, but in this case I'll make an exception. Lady's a little strong willed to say the least."

Summer had to laugh. "She's your perfect match."

Cassidy rolled her eyes. "That's what he said."

"He's right. Come on in while I get ready. It won't take me long."

A few minutes later she came back into the living room where Cassidy was stroking Hero and looking at the kittens. "They're still so tiny," she said.

"They are. Aren't they adorable?"

"What's adorable," said Cassidy, "is that man of yours. I just love that he took in a stray cat and helped deliver her babies. He looks like a big, mean, tough guy on the outside and on the inside he's just a big old softie."

Summer smiled. "He is, Cass. He's amazing."

Cassidy grinned. "Look at you! All gooey eyed. I'm so glad you and Autumn figured things out so that you can stay. Have you heard anything from her? How's she's getting on with setting up the tour?"

"I haven't spoken to her in a while. I need to call her." Summer was a little concerned. She didn't like not hearing from her sister. She was hoping everything was working out okay.

"Say hi from me when you do. Are you ready? Let's get going."

They stopped halfway down the steps. Another vehicle was coming up the driveway. "This is unbelievable," said Summer. "No one ever comes out here and now I have two visitors in one morning."

"Isn't that Beau's truck?" asked Cassidy.

"Oh." It was. Summer hoped he wasn't bringing James and Carly to have a look around. She'd assumed he'd call to set it up before he did that. It seemed like he was though, he wasn't alone in the truck.

Cassidy raised an eyebrow at her. "Did he not tell you he was coming?"

Summer shook her head.

Cassidy scowled. "That's just rude! Tell him he'll have to come back another time."

Summer knew that her friend would do just that. She couldn't bring herself to though. "I'd rather get it over with. You go on without me if you want."

"No way. I want to ride with you. I'll wait. But I tell you now, I'm not going to let them linger too long. Beau should have called first."

"I know, I know." Summer put a smile on her face as the truck came to a stop. Beau, Carly and James got out.

Then Summer heard a squeal. "Summer Breese!" Ruby shot out of the truck and came running toward her. She had to smile to herself. This should prove interesting, with Cassidy wanting her to hurry up and leave and Ruby no doubt wanting to stay. That could be a battle of wills to witness.

"Is your voice better yet? Can you sing me a song?" asked Ruby as she wrapped her arms around Summer's legs and smiled up at her.

Summer shook her head. "No, I can't sing for you, Ruby." Her voice still sounded raspy.

Beau looked concerned. "Are you okay? I hope you don't mind us just stopping by. We were on our way up the valley and I thought we'd stop on the off chance."

Carly gave her an apologetic look. "I'm sorry. We can come another time."

"It's okay," Summer said. "Beau did ask if you could come and take a look around. You may as well while you're here."

"We can't stay too long, though," Cassidy gave Beau a stern look. "We were just on our way out."

Summer smiled to herself. Cassidy wasn't going to just let it slide.

Beau wasn't going to let her get to him either. "We won't be long at all, thanks."

"Come on in then," said Summer.

Ruby let go of her legs and took hold of her hand as she walked up the steps.

Summer's phone rang as she opened the front door. It was Autumn. "I need to take this," she said to Beau. "Go right on in. It's not as if you don't know the place, is it?" She smiled at Cassidy who followed Beau and the others inside with a grim look on her face. Summer knew she wouldn't let them linger too long.

She walked back out onto the deck before she swiped to take the call.

"Hey, is everything okay?" She realized she'd answered in the same way Carter always did.

"I don't know. I'm hoping it will be, but I wanted to give you a heads up."

"About what?" Autumn sounded worried.

"That things aren't going as smoothly here as we'd assumed they would."

"Why what's going on?" Summer was worried now, too. She hoped things weren't going bad for her sister already.

"Ashley said there's no way McAdam Records would release you."

"Oh." Summer had only been worried about her sister. She hadn't even considered that this might be about her. "Why on earth would she say that? It's not what Clay said. And besides, it's not even something we need to think about for another couple of months yet."

Autumn sighed. "I know, but I was in her planning meeting for the next six months. She was talking about how to schedule a big comeback for you and how that would fit into the promotional calendar. I reminded her that we don't even know if you're going to be able to come back and she got really nasty. She doesn't believe you won't come back. I don't know what she's set up, but she seems to have a lot riding on you. She said even if you can't sing, you owe the company promo time and there's no way she won't get her money's worth from you."

Summer's heart sank. "Oh."

"I know. I'm going to do everything I can to change her mind, but I just wanted to warn you that whatever you've got going on with your cowboy, it looks like you can't leave Nashville completely just yet."

"I see."

"Is that what you were planning?"

Summer nodded, then remembered that she needed to actually speak. "Yeah." Her voice cracked again.

"You sound like crap by the way."

"Thanks."

"Sorry. I'm just surprised. You were doing so well when I was there."

"I was, but it seems to be worse than ever this morning."

"Well, I'll let you go then. I'll email you and we can talk that way."

"Okay. Is everything okay with you, though? With Matt's tour?"

Autumn sighed. "Yeah, everything's great. It's going to be awesome and I think that might be part of the problem. Matt was telling a couple of the guys what a great job I was doing and apparently Ashley has had a few more requests for me to work on tours and release campaigns. I think she doesn't like that I'm suddenly in demand and part of her wanting you back here is to make sure I'm kept busy on your stuff and not taking over anyone else's."

Summer frowned. "I don't get it. Why wouldn't she want you working with the other artists? Especially if you're doing such a good job?"

"Because I'm making her people look bad by comparison. It's a stupid business decision, but it's not about business. It's about her covering her own ass."

Summer sighed. There was so much of that in the industry. Good people got screwed over every day when they got in the way of someone else's ego or power trip. "You should talk to Clay."

Autumn sighed. "Ashley thought I might do that, she's already warned me off."

"She's a bitch!"

"Of the first order! Listen. You sound terrible and I need to get going. I'll email you."

"Okay, bye."

Summer hung up and looked down at Ruby who was tugging at her sleeve.

"Who's a bitch?"

Summer sighed. She didn't know the kid had been there listening! "What are you doing out here? I thought you were looking around the house."

Ruby pouted. "I didn't come to see the house. I came to see you!"

Summer forced a smile onto her face. "Thank you, it's nice to see you, too." She held out her hand and Ruby took it. "Let's go back in and see what they're doing, shall we?"

Ruby nodded and went with her. When they reached the front door, the others were just coming back out.

"Thanks," said Beau. "Told you we didn't need long."

Summer nodded. She was glad they were leaving.

Carly gave her an apologetic look and held her hand out to Ruby. "Come on."

Ruby shook her head. "I want to stay with Summer Breese!"

"I have to go myself now."

"Where are you going?"

"We have to go out," said Cassidy with an air of finality. She closed the front door behind them all and started down the steps. "And we're going to be late."

Ruby seemed a little taken aback and let Carly take her hand as they followed Cassidy.

Summer smiled and climbed into Cassidy's Tahoe. She was grateful that her friend was taking charge, she smiled at Ruby and waved at the others as Cassidy pulled away.

"Sorry if you think that was rude. I just wanted to get you out of there."

She shook her head. "I'm grateful. Thank you."

"What was the phone call? You don't look like it was good news."

Summer shook her head. She hadn't had time to fully process what her sister had told her yet—or what it might mean. "It was Autumn. Apparently the label isn't going to let me go. And it sounds as though things are getting difficult for her, too."

Cassidy looked across at her before she pulled out on East River Road. "And what does that mean? Will you have to go back to Nashville?"

Summer shrugged. "I don't know yet, but I hope not."

~ ~ ~

Carter sat in the office at the nursery and stared out the window. He was supposed to be taking inventory, but he kept letting his mind drift off. He was daydreaming! About him and Summer. He smiled, thinking about them having kids. About the life they could have together. He was finally allowing himself to believe—to get a bit carried away, if he was honest.

He looked up when he saw someone pulling up in the yard. It was Beau. Carter stood and went out to greet him. He had that couple with him again.

Beau grinned when he saw him. "Hey, Carter. You've met James and Carly, I believe?"

Carter tipped his hat at them. What did they want now?

"They're thinking they'd like to build rather than buy. We've been looking at some of the lots out at Cowboy Lake. Carly was curious about what kind of native landscaping possibilities there might be. I told her that's not my area of expertise, but the valley's ultimate authority happens to be my little brother."

Carly smiled at him. "I'm not even sure what questions I want to ask you yet. We haven't decided on a lot or anything, but when Beau said you had the nursery here, I just wanted to stop by and have a look around."

Carter nodded. "Feel free. And if you're really interested in native landscaping, then call me before you settle on a lot." He handed her his card. "If it's important to you, then you need to understand the possibilities before you buy a place that isn't going to be able to support your ideas."

She smiled. "Thank you."

Carter didn't know what else to say. They may become clients if they did end up buying somewhere, but for some reason they always made him feel uncomfortable. Maybe it was just because he saw them as a threat to Summer's privacy. He probably wasn't being fair. They seemed nice enough, but to him they represented the outside world, the fans, the pressure—everything that might take Summer away from him.

He looked up at a loud knock on the office door. It stood open and Shane peered around it, his hat coming first, followed by his big grin. "Hey guys. What is this, a family reunion?" He stopped when he saw Carly and James.

"Actually, it's business," said Beau.

Carter thought he could have been nicer about it, but Shane wasn't fazed anyway. Nothing much ever fazed him.

"It's okay," said James. "Good to see you, Shane."

"You, too. Have you decided on a place? Carter here is the man if you need landscaping. He's awesome. The grounds at the lodge are all his genius."

Carly smiled at Carter. "I was hoping so! I love what you've done there."

Carter smiled. He didn't really want his office to be the setting for social chit-chat.

"We haven't decided on a lot, yet," said James. "But we are thinking we're going to build. We stopped at Summer's place on the way up here. That would have been ideal, but we can build something just like it when we find the right spot."

Carter didn't like that they'd been out to Summer's place. She couldn't have had much notice. And he disliked the thought of them traipsing around her home, invading her space. "Well, give me a call when you know what you're thinking."

"We will. We're going to stay another week," said Carly. "We're hoping to find something and get the ball rolling before we have to leave."

"My mommy's coming, too," said Ruby who had been surprisingly quiet up till this point.

Shane perked up at that. He looked at Carly. "Do you think she might be interested in interviewing for a job while she's here?"

"I don't know. I mean she is looking for something, but I'm not sure she'd want to move up here."

"What did you have in mind?" asked James.

"Managing the lodge," Shane replied. "We're getting close to the busy season, and we're going to be expanding, too. From what I hear, she's experienced."

Carly nodded. "She is. I guess you can talk to her when she arrives. That additional room we booked is for her."

"Great," said Shane. "I'll look forward to meeting her."

Carter started to fiddle with his phone. He wanted them to leave now. He wanted to call Summer and check that she was okay after having her space invaded.

Shane caught his eye and understood. "Well, I need to get on my way. Are you guys headed back to the ranch? I can give you a ride if you like."

Beau shook his head. "We're heading up Deep Creek to look at a couple of lots up there. We should probably get going, too."

Carter walked them all to the door and tipped his hat as they left. He should be pleased at the prospect of a new-build job coming up, but he was more concerned with getting rid of them and calling Summer.

Once they'd gone he pulled his phone out of his back pocket and dialed her number.

She answered on the second ring. "Hi." Even with just that one syllable, he could tell her voice was bad.

"Are you okay?"

"I think so. Why, what's up?"

"Beau was just here with those people. He said they'd been to your place. I wanted to check you're okay?"

"I'm fine. It wasn't a problem. They didn't stay long."

"Only because I ran them off," called Cassidy.

Carter smiled to himself. He was grateful Cassidy was with her; she was as protective of Summer as he was. "Tell her I said thanks."

Summer laughed. "I will. I feel as though I have two bodyguards protecting me."

"You do," he said. "What are you two doing today?"

"We're on our way to the ranch. We're going to ride."

He smiled. He loved the idea that she would go out there to ride without him—just because she wanted to. "Well, be careful and have fun."

"We will. What time do you think you'll be home?"

"I should be done here around five today, but I was thinking I might hit the gym."

"You should, you don't get in there as much as you'd like, and that's my fault."

"It's not your fault, it's my choice. Even if I go I'll be back by six thirty."

"Great, I'll see you when you get there; but don't rush, will you?"

"I can't promise that. I need a workout, but I need to see you." He had to wonder though, even aside from her voice being bad, she didn't sound quite right. "Is everything okay?"

"I hope so. I talked to Autumn. Things aren't looking good."

His heart rate quickened at that. "Why, what's going on?"

"I'll tell you about it tonight. We just arrived at the ranch."

"Okay. I love you, see you later."

"Love you, too."

Chapter Nineteen

Summer closed her laptop and stared out the window. She'd enjoyed riding out with Cassidy, but she hadn't been able to relax completely. She'd been too worried about her sister. Since she'd come home she'd spent most of her time emailing with her, trying to figure out what was going on and what they could do about it.

From what Autumn had said in her email it was almost as though Ashley was blackmailing her! Summer's first thought with all of this was that they just needed to talk to Clay. He'd clear it all up. He'd specifically told Summer that if the day ever came when they both knew she wasn't coming back, that it'd all be okay. Ashley seemed to disagree though. She'd told Autumn that she'd better not go running to Clay to back her up. Ashley ran PR for him, and according to her, she got the final say. It sounded as though she wanted Summer back, and she wanted Autumn back working with her. It seemed that the real problem was that Ashley had hired some of her old cronies from her previous label and they hadn't been doing a great job. Now that Autumn was treading on their toes, Ashley didn't like it—didn't like having her own people look bad in comparison.

Summer shook her head. She knew Clay wouldn't see it that way. He wanted the best people for the job, no matter what the job. She'd toured with him in the past and knew that was the case. He didn't care about egos or rule books or industry standards; he just cared that he had the right person to do the best job in every position. She wanted to call him and tell him what Ashley was up to, but she didn't dare. Ashley had threatened Autumn that she'd make sure her name was as good as mud if she went over her head and talked to Clay.

So it seemed that Autumn was stuck in a lose-lose situation. Ashley was blocking her from working with other artists and blocking her from doing anything about it. She was being backed into a corner where the only artist she'd be able to work with was Summer herself. Except Summer didn't want to work anymore.

She sighed again. Just when she'd thought she could walk away from her career without it affecting her sister. She didn't know what to do to make it right. All she could think of was to call Clay, but she just didn't dare do it.

She smiled when she heard Carter running up the front steps. She might have had a few surprise visitors today, but she didn't doubt this was him. He wasn't exactly light-footed, and it was six-thirty, exactly when he'd said he'd be home. She was glad he'd managed to fit in a trip to the gym. She smiled at the memory of meeting Melanie at his house. She knew she didn't have anything to worry about there. Melanie might have been interested in him, but she'd backed right off when she met Summer. And she didn't think for a minute that Carter was interested in Melanie. He made it very clear, at every opportunity that he was in love with Summer.

The front door opened and he came striding in. He took her breath away whenever she laid eyes on him. He was so big, so muscular, and such a sweetheart! He came and leaned in the doorway and smiled at her. "How are you feeling? How's your voice?" She nodded. "It's okay." It was obvious that it wasn't though. He came to her and leaned down on the desk to kiss her. "It doesn't sound it."

She shrugged. "There's not a lot I can do about it."

"Except rest it. I don't suppose you managed to do that today, either."

She shrugged again. Between talking to Autumn, having Carly and James over, and then spending the afternoon with Cassidy, she hadn't really.

He surprised her when he scooped her up out of her chair and carried her through to the living room with a smile.

She reached her arms up around his neck and smiled back. She loved the way he picked her up and carried her around like this.

"Well, tonight you rest. You're going to sit right here on the sofa and I'm going to take care of dinner."

She raised an eyebrow at him in surprise.

He gave her a sheepish grin. "It won't be exactly gourmet, but hopefully I'll get extra points for sentimentality. I got us frozen pizza and ice cream on the way back from the gym."

She kissed him on the lips. "Lots of extra points," she croaked.

He frowned and put her down on the sofa. "Do you think it's stress that makes it worse?"

She thought about it. Sometimes it seemed as though it was stress that caused it, but she'd started croaking again before any of today's stress had started. She shook her head.

He didn't look convinced. "How about I go get the pizza started and you write down what's going on with Autumn for me?"

"Okay." She did want to talk to him about it. Mostly she wanted him to know that she might have to go back to Nashville, for a little while at least. She needed him to understand why, and that it wasn't because she wanted to. She'd made up her mind she wanted to be here, wanted to be with him, and she wanted to be sure he really understood that. The way her voice felt she wasn't going to be able to say it all, so she'd probably better start writing.

He went to fetch her purse from the counter and handed it to her. "I'm guessing your pad is in there, though how you'll ever find it in there is beyond me."

She made a face at him and opened her purse to start rummaging inside it.

He grinned. "Don't fall in. If you're not out of there in twenty minutes I'm sending a search party after you."

She laughed. Why did everyone have to tease her about her purse? She liked to carry what she needed with her. That was all. She pulled her pad out and set it on the coffee table. This was going to be a long note.

When she'd finished she read it back through. She seemed to have covered everything. She wondered if Carter would be able to see anything that she couldn't. She was pretty sure he'd think like she did. That she needed to talk to Clay and straighten things out. But the catch there was that Ashley would know and she would make Autumn's life hell over it. Ashley wasn't an easy person to deal with. Summer had been glad that Autumn ran things for her; their situation was a little different than most of the other artists. But if she wasn't part of the deal anymore, Autumn would be at Ashley's mercy. She had a special say in Summer's case, but she wouldn't have with any other artists she worked with.

Carter came back in and sat down beside her. "The pizza won't be long, and I opened a bottle of cab to let it breathe."

Summer smiled. Carter would just as soon have a beer as a glass of wine, but he'd learned what she liked and tried to give it to her when he could.

"Thanks." She reached up and kissed his cheek.

"You're welcome." He reached for the pad then looked up to check with her. "Can I?"

She nodded, then waited while he read.

He had a frown on his face by the time he finished. "This Ashley sounds like a piece of work. What's her deal?"

Summer shrugged. "Power? Control? Not being shown up that the people she brought on board aren't that great. Clay likes to have the best people, no matter if they're singing or sweeping the floor. He always wants the best people doing the best job. That's what his label is all about."

Carter pursed his lips. "Can't you just talk to him?"

"I want to. But I don't know what it would mean for Autumn."

"I don't get that. What could Ashley do? If Clay says you're fine to leave and Autumn's good to work with other singers, what could Ashley do about it?"

Summer sighed. "Make Autumn's life miserable. She's done it before, to one of the execs that worked there before she arrived. She spread all kinds of lies. Ruined his name. He left town in the end. No one wanted to work with him, and he hadn't done a thing wrong. Just crossed Ashley. I can't let that happen to Autumn." Her voice was barely a whisper by the time she'd finished.

Carter nodded slowly. "You're right. There's no way you can let your sister suffer."

He had an odd look on his face. Summer didn't like it, not one bit. "What are you thinking?"

He shook his head. "That the pizza needs to come out and you need to quit talking."

She watched him make his way into the kitchen. His whole demeanor had changed, but she didn't get why.

He came back with two glasses of wine and she smiled up at him. "Did I do something wrong?"

He shook his head. "No, darlin'. But I think I might have."

What on earth did that mean? He was gone before she could ask, but returned with the pizza and two plates. He set everything down on the coffee table and served her a slice.

"Carter, what is it?"

He shook his head. "I'm just worried about your sister, that's all."

Now, Summer thought she understood—and it worried her. Family was everything to him and she knew he wouldn't want Autumn to suffer in any way.

She put a hand on his arm. "It'll all work out. It'll be okay. I might have to go back, but it won't be for long."

He nodded sadly. "It'll all work out for the best."

She didn't like the way he said that. "What do you mean?"

He smiled at her, but it didn't reach his eyes. "What I say. Now will you give your voice a rest and eat? I slaved over that for you."

She gave him a smile as weak as his joke. She had a nasty feeling he was shutting down on her.

~ ~ ~

Carter lay awake and stared out at the moon. Summer slept peacefully beside him. She was so beautiful with her long blonde hair spread around her on the pillow. Her little arm stretched across his waist. He wanted to touch her, stroke her hair, but he didn't dare; he didn't want to wake her.

They'd had a quiet evening, eating ice cream and watching movies. They hadn't talked much, but that was mostly because he wanted her to rest her voice. It didn't sound good at all. He hadn't wanted to talk himself, because he didn't know what to say. He hated the thought of Autumn getting screwed over because of him. Well, he knew it wasn't exactly his fault. It wasn't really because of him. It was because Summer wanted to be with him. He sighed and shifted a little, careful not to disturb her.

He couldn't see any solutions though. If this Ashley woman was determined to keep Autumn down, he didn't know what they could do about it. From what Summer had explained, the only avenue for Autumn to continue working was to manage Summer. If Summer wasn't there, then Autumn had nothing left to do. But if Summer couldn't sing anyway? He didn't know. What he did know was that Summer would be miserable if Autumn was out of a job. Could she work with a different label? He didn't know the answer to that. He had a feeling that this Ashley wouldn't make life easy for her no matter what she did. Unless she brought Summer back and stayed away from other artists. He had to wonder why she wanted Summer back so badly. He understood that she wouldn't want to lose one of her biggest names, but if Summer couldn't sing, she couldn't sing. His head was going around in circles. He didn't understand most of it. What did he know about the music industry anyway? One thing he did understand was the bond between siblings. He would never do a thing that might hurt any of his brothers. He couldn't let Summer hurt her sister just so she could be with him. He couldn't lie here any longer. He carefully moved Summer's arm and slid out of bed.

He got a drink of water and went to check on Hero. She was curled up in the bed Summer had bought for her, her kittens nestled into her side. He had to smile. They lived like royalty since they'd moved down here. Hero blinked at him and purred. He scratched her ear and sat down beside the bed.

He didn't know what to do, but he felt like he had to do something. He sighed. He did know one solution that would work, but he couldn't bring himself to do it. If he were to go to Nashville with Summer, then everything would be okay. Except, *he* wouldn't be okay. He wouldn't be able to leave the valley, his work, his life, his family. He wouldn't survive and he knew it. If he moved there to be with her, he'd be miserable. Just like she'd be miserable if she stayed here with him and it cost her sister her career. He loved her too much to do that to her. He knew what he had to do now.

He had to let her go.

His shoulders slumped. Who had he been kidding anyway? He was a lucky bastard to have spent so much time with her. He must have been crazy to have been thinking about forever with her—thinking about asking her to marry him. He'd gotten carried away. He knew better. He'd be grateful for what they'd shared—it was more than he ever could have hoped for—but he had to let her go. She might not see it now, but she'd thank him for it someday. They were from different worlds and he should have remembered that from the start. Hero looked up at him as he sat there in the darkness and one big fat tear rolled down his cheek.

Chapter Twenty

Carter had already left when Summer woke up. That was strange. Even when he had to get off to work really early, he always spooned her before he got out of her bed, kissed her neck, told her how much he loved her.

She got up, slipped her robe on and went into the kitchen. He was gone. She peered out the window. Yep. His truck was gone. She was worried. He'd gone really quiet after they'd talked about Autumn last night. She hadn't missed his reaction when she'd said she'd have to go back to Nashville. Did he think she'd leave? He was crazy if he did! She wouldn't survive without him. He'd become so much a part of her in the short time they'd been together. She couldn't imagine her life without him. She didn't want to. He was everything.

She went back to the kitchen and unplugged her phone that had been charging on the counter. She hit the speed dial and waited. It rang and rang, but he didn't pick up. Instead it went to voicemail.

"Carter, please call me back? I can't believe you left without saying good-bye." Her voice sounded terrible. "Call me. I love you."

She hung up and went to get a glass of water. She stood in the
kitchen wringing her hands together. She might be
overreacting to the fact that he'd left for work without saying
good-bye, but it felt so much worse than that. He'd left when
something was troubling him, and he hadn't wanted to talk to
her. The last time he'd felt that he'd caused problems between
her and Autumn, he'd taken off—and hadn't come back! At
least not until she'd left. Surely he wasn't doing that now? He
wouldn't just leave without talking to her—would he?

She stared at her phone, but it didn't ring. She took a deep
breath to steady herself. She was being silly. She needed to go
take a shower and get herself dressed and ready for the day—
whatever the day might hold.

He still hadn't called her back by the time she was dressed.
Now she was getting really worried. She tried him again, but it
went straight to voicemail. She didn't leave a message this
time. He knew she wanted to talk to him. Instead she called
Cassidy.

"Hey, chica."

"Hi. I don't suppose you or Shane have heard from Carter this
morning have you?"

"Uh-oh. What's up? He did stop by here early this morning.
Shane was on his way out and I wasn't even dressed. They
talked outside. Why, what's going on?"

"Maybe nothing. I don't know. But I need to talk to him and
he's not answering me. He left before I woke up, and he
wasn't right last night."

"What wasn't he right about?"

"Ugh. All the stuff with Autumn. I think he thinks it's all his
fault."

"How could anything to do with Autumn be his fault?"

"Because if I was still there, Autumn would be fine. The reason I'm not there is because I'm here with him."

"That's not true though, is it? You don't want to sing anymore. That's got nothing to do with being with him."

"No, but *he* doesn't get that. All he sees is that I'm staying here because of him. I'm scared that he's taken off again."

Cassidy sighed. "Sit tight. You sound like shit. I'm coming over. It might all be nothing, but I'd rather you were writing this down than speaking."

"Thanks." Summer's throat felt as though it was closing up. She didn't know what Cassidy could do, any more than she knew what she herself could do, but it would be good to have her friend here.

~ ~ ~

Cassidy grabbed her car keys and pulled her cell phone out to call Shane.

"What did Carter want this morning?" she asked when he picked up.

"Hello, my love, how nice of you to call to see how I'm doing."

She laughed. "Asshole! I'm sorry, okay? I'm worried. Summer just called me in a panic because he took off without saying anything this morning."

"Ah."

"Ah, what? What does that mean? He's not headed for the hills again, is he?"

"Not yet."

"Oh, shit. What's his deal?"

"He doesn't want to screw things up for Summer and her sister. He thinks if he takes himself out of the picture she'll go back to Nashville and everything will be okay."

Cassidy sighed. "Except Summer would be heart broken."

"And so would he."

"And Autumn would feel like shit that they broke up because of her."

"Yup. I did try to tell him all of that this morning, you know."

"But you didn't get through?"

"He's shut down."

"But he hasn't left?"

"No, but he's thinking about it."

"So what do we do?"

Shane was quiet for a long moment.

"What?"

"I don't know. I mean, is it really our place to do anything? I want to help them out, but I don't want to interfere."

"Shane! We have to do something!"

"I had a feeling you might say that, but what exactly do we do? I'm open to suggestions."

Cassidy thought about it. "Do we go find him and try to talk some sense into him?"

"Only if you want him to hightail it out of town."

She sighed.

"Listen, why don't you go see Summer? I'll see if I can catch up with Carter."

"Okay, thanks. Call me when you know anything?"

"Will do."

Cassidy hung up and headed for her car. She wasn't sure that they'd accomplished anything. Shane had already talked to Carter this morning. She still wasn't sure she really understood what was going on with Autumn that meant Summer should go back to Nashville anyway. She decided to call her before she went to Summer's place, to see if she could get a clearer picture of what was going on.

"Hey, Cassidy." Autumn sounded surprised to hear from her.

"Hey. Is everything okay with you?"

Autumn sighed. "No, but don't tell my sister that."

"What's going on?"

"Ashley's trying to run me out. She doesn't like that I'm working so well with Matt. I think she sees me as a threat, so she's trying to keep me locked down to only working with Summer."

"And she doesn't like the fact that Summer's not going to be there for you to work with?"

"Not one bit. She's trying to make sure she comes back whether she can sing or not. Is she okay? She sounded terrible when I talked to her."

"She's not okay, but not just her voice. Carter seems to have gotten it into his head that he's screwing things up for the two of you. He thinks the best thing he can do is take himself out of the picture so Summer can come back to Nashville."

Autumn gave a harsh laugh. "That wouldn't solve anything. It wouldn't bring Summer's voice back. It wouldn't get Ashley off my case, but it would break Summer's heart. She's head over heels in love with the guy. Can he not see that?"

"I think he's a little too caught up in being head over heels in love with her. He'd do anything for her. Including giving her up so she doesn't have to choose between you and him."

Autumn blew out a big sigh. "Can you talk some sense into him?"

"Maybe, if I can find him."

"Should I come back up there and tell him myself?"

"It sounds like you've got enough going on."

"I have, but this is important. Summer's finally met a guy she wants to spend her life with. No way am I going to see her lose him because of me."

Cassidy had to laugh. "Now you sound just like him!"

"Oh, shit. I've got Ashley on the other line. I've got to go. Call me later, will you?"

"Sure."

"And, Cassidy, thanks."

"No problem."

Cassidy stood there looking at her phone. She'd talked to everyone but the man in question. She wondered if Carter would pick up if she called.

She decided to give it a try.

"Hi Cassidy, is everything okay?"

She had to smile. He couldn't override his instincts if he wanted to! "I'm okay, I'm worried about you though."

"There's no need. I'm fine."

"Are you really? Or are you about to make a big dumb mistake?" Cassidy felt a twinge of guilt using those words. They were the words he used so often about himself, but that was why she said them—in the hopes of getting through to him.

"What do you mean?"

"You know damned well what I mean. Are you about to walk away from Summer because you think that's what's best for her?"

He didn't reply.

"Well, I can tell you right now, that isn't what's best for her. You'd break her heart, Carter."

"But, Cassidy, staying with me would break her heart in a different way because it would hurt her sister. I can't do that to her."

"Sorry, Carter, but I don't think that's your choice to make."

"What do you mean?"

"I mean you can't just make her decisions for her and walk out on her."

Carter was quiet for a long moment.

"Are you still there?"

"Yeah."

"So what are you going to do?"

"I don't know."

"Well, how about you start by calling Summer? She's one upset little lady right now and I think she's waiting to hear from you."

Carter sighed. "Okay."

Cassidy smiled, relieved.

"Can I ask you something?"

"Anything."

"What would you do, Cassidy, if you were me?"

Wow! It was easy, from where she was standing, to tell him he had to find another way to deal with this, but what *would* she do, if she were in his shoes? She knew the answer. "I'd probably screw things up completely."

"How?"

"Never mind. I'm not going there. This one's for you to fix or screw up all by yourself."

"Thanks."

~ ~ ~

Carter hung up and put his phone back in his pocket. He didn't know what the hell to do! He closed up the greenhouse and went back to the house. He'd called the guys and told them he wouldn't be on the job this morning. They were at a stage where they could get on without him for a couple of days. He'd come back home needing to hole up and think. The only solution he could see was to take himself out of the picture, but he didn't want to. The way he saw it Summer would have to choose between him and Autumn and he didn't want her to have to do that. He wouldn't make her do that. He went out to the shed and set out several bowls of food and water for the cats. Buster came and rubbed around his legs.

"I might be gone a few days, old fella," Carter said as he scratched the cat's ears.

Buster turned big green eyes on him and meowed loudly.

To Carter it sounded as though he was disagreeing. He shook his head—it must just be his own instincts disagreeing really. He closed up the shed and went to collect his gym bag. Whenever he needed to think, he hit the gym. It helped somehow. It should be quiet in there on a weekday morning. There'd be no one to disturb him and maybe inspiration would strike while he was lifting.

He pulled up in the gym's parking lot and pulled his bag out. He'd told Cassidy he'd call Summer, but he didn't know what to say to her. He pulled his phone out and sent her a quick text.

I love you.

That was the only thing he knew for certain right now.

He was halfway through his workout when he saw Melanie. Damn. He didn't want to talk to anyone at all right now, and if he did it wouldn't be her.

She smiled and came over.

"It's unusual to see you in here in the day," she said. "How are you doing?"

He pursed his lips. "Not great. That's why I'm here. I need some time and space to think, I figured this might be the place to find it." He didn't want to be rude, but he didn't want to talk to her either.

"Is everything okay with you and Summer?"

He sighed, he sure as hell didn't want to tell her about that! He shrugged.

"I don't mean to pry, Carter. I just want to see you happy. She seems so nice. I want things to work out for the two of you."

"So do I."

She held his gaze for a long moment. "I know it's none of my business, but hiding out in here isn't going to fix whatever's wrong."

That stung, because he knew it was true. "I don't know what is going to fix it, though."

"Well, usually when two people have problems they need to talk to each other before anything gets fixed."

Carter sighed. "The problems aren't between me and her, though. It's all about other people."

Melanie nodded. "Well then maybe you need to talk to the other people?" She touched his arm. "Sorry. It really is none of my business. I just hope you can sort it all out. Good luck."

"Thanks."

He watched her walk away and climb onto one of the bikes. She put her headphones in and gave him a little smile before she started to peddle.

Carter sat on the bench and thought about what she'd said. If he were to talk to the other people, who exactly would that be? Autumn? What could he say to her? This Ashley person? He couldn't see himself convincing some high powered music executive of anything. He shuddered at the thought. Other than Summer, he didn't do well talking to women from the city. He did better with men from the country. Then it hit him. He knew what he had to do.

~ ~ ~

Summer rolled her eyes at Cassidy. She could hardly speak anymore. She knew now that the stress was making her throat worse. She also knew there was nothing she'd be able to do about it until she talked to Carter.

She held up her pad.

What do I do???

Cassidy shrugged. "I wish I could tell you. I don't think there's much you can do until you hear from him.

But what if I don't? She scrawled.

"Well, he can't stay gone forever. I guess you just have to sit it out."

If he thinks I'm going to leave, he's got another thing coming. I'm staying right here.

"Hopefully he'll come to his senses and come home and talk to you."

Summer nodded. She hoped so, but she was starting to have a really bad feeling about all this. The worst part was that she had no control over any of it. She wanted to *do* something. She wanted to do something for Autumn. She wanted to do something to make Carter see sense, but there was nothing she could do. Except wait.

Cassidy's phone rang.

"Have you spoken to him?"

Summer assumed it must be Shane.

"Oh."

"*What?*" Summer's voice was barely a whisper, but she had to know!

Cassidy looked up at her. "Well call me when you know anything, will you?"

She hung up.

"Now he's not answering Shane's calls either. Shane went out to the courthouse, and Carter's crew said they're not expecting him today. So Shane went to the nursery and there's no sign of him there or at the house either."

Summer sighed. "You think he's gone?"

Cassidy shrugged. "I don't know, but I do know you need to stop talking and start writing.

Summer's phone beeped and she snatched it up. It was a text from Carter.

I love you.

That was all it said, but it made her heart leap. At least he'd sent something. At least he hadn't shut down completely on her.

I love you too. Please come home.

She wanted to say so much more than that, but there was no point in a text. She needed him to come back, to talk to face to face, and to figure out how they were going to handle this.

Cassidy raised an eyebrow at her.

She shrugged. "He loves me," she whispered.

Cassidy smiled. "Then he'd better start proving it."

Chapter Twenty-One

Carter sat in the departure lounge and looked around at all the people waiting to board. He was glad that he only needed to go as far as Salt Lake City. That had been a lucky break. He didn't like to fly and the thought of flying all the way to Nashville had filled him with dread. A quick google search had told him that he didn't need to go there anyway. The person he needed to talk to was in Salt Lake tonight, for one night only.

His phone rang and he sighed. Whoever it was, he didn't want to talk to them. He checked the display. Cassidy. He reluctantly swiped to answer.

"Thanks for picking up."

He had to smile. "I just figured it'd be easier to answer now, than to take the grief later."

She laughed. "Glad we understand each other. Do you want to tell me where you are and what you're doing?"

"Not really."

"Tell me anyway?"

He sighed. "I'm at the airport, waiting to get on a plane." He heard her suck her breath in sharply. "I'm not just taking off. You were the one who told me that it's for me to fix this or screw it up all by myself. I'm going to try to fix it...But I'm afraid I might just screw it all up."

"Want to tell me where you're going?"

"No. Listen, I have to go. They're calling my flight. Take care of Summer for me."

"I will, but when you get back here..."

"I know. I have to go. Bye."

He hung up and joined the line at the gate. He hoped to hell that he wasn't about to screw this up. If things went like he hoped, then he'd be fixing things for Summer and himself—and for Autumn too. If they didn't, he might screw things up, and then Summer might just hate him for it. He couldn't afford to think about that. Now that he'd decided what he needed to do, he had to believe it would all work out. It was a gamble, and he wasn't normally one to gamble on anything, but in this case the stakes were so high he couldn't afford not to.

~ ~ ~

Summer sat out on the deck. She couldn't settle down to anything. She couldn't believe that Carter had left. Cassidy had reassured her that he hadn't said he was taking off, but still. Where was he? What *was* he doing? And why wouldn't he talk to her?

She sighed. She knew she wasn't going to get answers to any of those questions until she saw him. Hero came out onto the deck and sat in a patch of sunshine beside her. This was the first time Summer had seen her leave her kittens to do more than go to the bathroom. She reached down to stroke her. Hero purred and jumped up onto her knee. She head butted Summer's shoulder and kneaded her lap. It was comforting in a way Summer couldn't explain. If she was honest, she'd grown used to the thought that she and Carter would live here, in this wonderful house. They'd have Hero and her kittens and become a real little family. At some point they'd have little ones of their own. Now, in the face of it all going up in flames, she could admit it to herself. She'd had it set in her own mind that this was going to be her life—Carter was her future. She wasn't too concerned if she never sang again. She'd found where she belonged and the man she belonged with.

She couldn't stand the thought of having it all torn away from her. As if sensing Summer's discomfort at that thought, Hero jumped back down and went back inside to her kittens.

Her phone buzzed with a text. It was Autumn.

Are you okay?

Yeah. Carter's gone, but Cass says he isn't running. I don't know what to think. Or what to do.

Apparently Autumn didn't know what to say either. It was a long few minutes before she replied.

I don't want either of you to worry about me. I can walk away from McAdam.

Summer sighed. She didn't want Autumn to sacrifice herself any more than she wanted Carter to.

No you won't! I'll come back for a while. Don't let her run you out.

There was another long pause.

She can't run our lives. Screw her! I'll walk away.

Summer shook her head. Autumn was stubborn. She'd sooner walk away from her career than have someone use it against her. But Summer couldn't let her do that.

Let's both sleep on it? Maybe we'll think of something.

She could imagine Autumn's face as she read that. She hated to wait. She would want to make a decision and get on with it.

Ok. I'll call you in the morning.

Summer wanted to feel relieved, but a part of her was concerned that when Autumn did call it would be to say that she'd already quit. She put her phone away and got up to go inside. Then she came outside again. She didn't know what to do with herself.

~ ~ ~

As Carter walked toward the stadium, he had to wonder if this wasn't the dumbest move he'd ever made. How was he even going to get to see the guy, let alone convince him that he didn't need Summer back—and that he did need Autumn? He decided his best bet would be to hang out by the back entrance. That was how it worked, wasn't it? The singers and the band would come around here. He realized when he rounded the corner of the building that he wasn't alone in hoping to catch more than a glimpse of Clay McAdam. There was a barrier set up by the doors and maybe thirty people were hanging around. He pushed his way through to where two big burly guys stood guarding the door.

One of them eyed him suspiciously. "What do you want?"

Carter tipped his hat. "Is there any way I could have a word with Clay McAdam?"

The guy laughed. "You're kidding, right?"

Carter shook his head. He couldn't be more serious.

"Listen, every single one of these people would love to have a word with Clay. It doesn't work like that. You go take your seat in the stadium and you can hear him sing. That's as close as you're going to get."

"But I need to talk to him."

The guy shook his head. "Forget it." He turned away from Carter as the door opened behind him. His walkie-talkie crackled and he spoke into it. "Okay folks," he called. "We're going to need all of you to move over to the other side, if you will. Clay's on his way in and if you're all out of the way there may be time for autographs."

Carter moved with the rest of the group as the two doormen lifted the barriers and corralled them all on the other side of the street. His heart was racing. Here came his chance and he couldn't afford to miss it.

A black Suburban came around the corner and the small crowd went wild. They were mostly women, and Carter's ears rang with their screaming as the Suburban's door opened and Clay McAdam got out. He took his hat off and waved it toward his fans with a grin. "Now that's what I call a welcome," he said.

Carter had to keep pushing his way to the front as excited women tried to elbow him out of the way, all wanting to get an autograph or touch Clay's arm. Carter had never understood this kind of reaction. He hated the thought of Summer being treated this way. Clay stopped to sign a program that the woman beside Carter thrust in front of him.

"Mr. McAdam?" said Carter.

He didn't even look up, as he signed a shirt and continued chatting and smiling. Carter stepped forward and spoke up. "Mr. McAdam. Sir?" he had to shout to make himself heard, but it had the desired effect. Clay looked up and met his gaze.

"Nice to meet you, son. Thanks for coming."

Carter didn't have anything for him to sign, so he held his hand out to shake.

Clay hesitated, then reached out. He seemed to be weighing Carter up, as if there was something about him he wasn't sure of. When he took Carter's hand, Carter gripped on tight. "Sir, I need to talk to you."

Clay immediately tried to pull his hand away, but Carter held on. He had no choice, this would be his only chance.

"It's about Summer."

Clay's eyebrows came together and he stared hard at Carter, then there was a flicker of recognition in his eyes. "I thought you looked familiar, son!"

Carter grinned with relief.

Now it was Clay who was gripping his hand and pulling him toward the gap between the barriers. When they reached it he pulled him through and out of the crowd of now grumbling women.

"Sorry ladies," called Clay. "I hope y'all enjoy the show. I'll try and catch you later." He grinned at Carter. "For now I need to catch up with an old friend."

Carter grinned at the doorman who looked stunned as Clay pulled him in through the door.

Once they were up in the dressing room, Clay asked one of the many people milling around to get them both a beer. Then he took a seat and gestured for Carter to do the same.

Carter perched on the edge of the sofa. His plan had only gone as far as somehow getting to talk to Clay. Now he was here, he wasn't at all sure what he was going to say.

"So, what can I do for you, son?"

Carter swallowed. He wasn't exactly sure what Clay could do for him. All he'd known was that he needed to talk to him.

Clay smiled gently. "Is she okay?"

Carter nodded. "She is. I'm sorry to do this to you, sir…"

"Call me Clay. You may as well. I've a feeling we're going to be friends."

Carter thought he was saying that to put him at ease, but it only made him more nervous. He hoped Clay wasn't expecting him to move to Nashville with Summer. "Thank you, sir. Err, Clay."

Clay waited while he gathered his thoughts.

"Summer's okay. She's happy...*we're* happy. In Montana."

Clay nodded. "I never expected her to come back, kid. When that story ran in the papers up there I saw the photos of the two of you together. I knew."

Wow! Carter hadn't been expecting that.

"So, what's the problem?"

"Autumn."

Clay frowned. "Autumn will do just fine. In fact from what I hear, she already is. She's whipping Matt's tour into place and..."

Carter decided to go for it. "And someone named Ashley doesn't like it. She's saying Autumn needs to bring Summer back, and she doesn't want her working with the other singers."

Clays eyebrows came together again. He was a good-looking guy; even Carter could see it, but he looked pretty imposing when he frowned like that.

"And why hasn't Summer come to me herself?"

"Because, sir, this Ashley is threatening to make sure no one will want to work with Autumn if either of them go bothering you with any of this. From what I understand, she's got her own people working PR for your singers and she doesn't like the fact—and doesn't want you to discover that—Autumn does a much better job than any of them. Summer once told me that you like to have the best people on every job, no matter what job it is. I thought you should know what's going on. I can't let this Ashley blackmail the girls. I can't let her make a fool out of you." He hesitated, but he had to say it—had to be honest. "And most of all I can't let her steal my future with Summer."

"How could she do that?"

"Before I came to see you. I'd almost decided to walk away from Summer. To make sure that she went back to Nashville, to help her sister out. I didn't want her to have to ruin her sister's career in order to be with me."

Clay nodded slowly. "And if I tell you you're full of it? If I say that Ashley has my full support, then what?"

Carter's heart sank. "Then I guess I have to thank you for your time, and I have to live with the fact that I just screwed everything up for both of them." He got to his feet.

"Hold up, son. I don't think you're full it. I think you've got guts. I've had a bad feeling about Ashley for a little while now. I misjudged there, and I'm not afraid to admit it. You've got balls, kid, but then love will do that to a guy, huh?" He smiled. "Don't you worry about a thing. I'm going to have to get ready and get out there, but will you do me favor?"

"What's that?"

"Stick around. After tonight's show I have forty-eight hours before the next one in Seattle. We've got some fixing to do, you and me."

Carter felt the relief rush through him. He nodded and took a swig of the beer that had been placed on the table beside him. "Thank you."

Clay grinned as he got up. "No, thank *you*. I think we're all going to come out winners in this one."

Chapter Twenty-Two

Summer felt awful when she woke up. She'd hardly slept at all. She wasn't used to sleeping by herself anymore. She hadn't been able to get comfortable without Carter to rest her head on. She missed him so much. And she was worried. She was worried where he might be, worried what he might be doing. Most of all she was worried that she might have to get used to sleeping without him. She didn't want to have to do that. Ever. She got up and went to make herself a pot of coffee. She wasn't supposed to drink too much of the stuff, but she needed it this morning. She checked her phone. There was a text from Carter. It had come in at one o'clock in the morning.

I love you. I'm coming home.

She smiled and heaved a sigh of relief. Once he was here they could talk. They could figure out what to do together. It would all be okay. Even as she thought it, the knot clenched in her stomach. Would it, though? If they decided that everything would be okay for them, would that mean everything would be far from okay for Autumn? She hated the thought that doing what made her happy might cost her sister her career. She wanted to believe that Autumn could walk away and go to work with someone else. Ashley said she could ruin her reputation and make sure she never worked in Nashville again, but did she really have that much sway? Summer knew how it worked, though. Ashley didn't need that much sway. All she needed was to start a rumor. Gossip spread fast in Nashville. If people in the industry thought there was a reason that McAdam Records had parted ways with Autumn, they wouldn't want to take the risk of working with her themselves. She needed to call Autumn. They'd said they'd sleep on it. Summer still didn't have a solution, but she was starting to think she'd have to go back to Nashville to try to sort things out. Maybe Carter would go with her? Just for a short time. As she considered that possibility, a thought struck her. If she made Beau an offer on the house and got started on the purchasing process, surely that would help Carter to see that she wasn't going to let him give up on her—on them? It would show him she was serious about staying here, even if she had to go away for a short time. That was it. She needed to buy the house!

For the first time since she'd woken up yesterday, she felt as though there was something constructive she could do. She took her coffee and her phone and went to sit on the sofa to call Beau.

"Good morning," he answered. He sounded bright and perky, almost overly so.

"Hi, Beau." Her voice sounded a little better this morning, but not much.

"Ouch, you sound bad. Are you okay?"

"I'm fine. I want to talk to you about buying the house."

"Oh."

That sounded ominous. "What's up? You did say I could have first refusal, didn't you?"

"I did, but things have changed."

"What do you mean they've changed?" Summer couldn't believe it. She knew the others said that Beau could be an asshole if he wanted to be, but she hadn't wanted to believe it. She'd never seen that in him, until now.

"I'm sorry, Summer. Last night I received an offer on the place, and it's not one I can refuse."

Wow! She was stunned. "I didn't think you'd do that to me, Beau!"

"Neither did I. I'm sorry, Summer." He did sound genuinely sorry, but that didn't count for much.

"So am I," she said and hung up. She couldn't quite believe it. He was going to sell the place out from under her? She supposed she should have asked him when he wanted her out, but she'd been too stunned. Besides, it'd be up to him to tell her. She was only renting month to month, but she'd assumed—because he'd said—that it would be for as long as she liked.

She sat and fumed to herself as she drank her coffee. She got her phone out and started browsing the real estate sites. She was staying here in the valley, no matter what Beau or Carter or anyone else said or did! She'd just have to find another place. She wanted Carter to know that she was ready to put down roots here, and buying a house should go a long way toward proving that to him.

She could only imagine that Carly and James had made an overpriced offer on this place. And Beau was too greedy to turn it down—even if it meant going back on his word. Well, screw him! She'd just find another house and work with a different realtor.

She browsed through a couple of websites before she had to admit that she was putting off calling Autumn. She dialed her number and waited, but only got through to voicemail. "Hey, sis. We need to decide what we're going to do. Call me back."

She hung up and looked around. She'd be sad to leave this house. She'd loved it since the first time she saw it. It had felt like a sanctuary and she'd been thinking that it would become her and Carter's home. Oh, well. She'd adapt. She'd have to. She'd find some place just as good, if not better.

She wanted to call Carter to see where he was and when he'd be back. She hoped that going off by himself like that had been enough to make him come to his senses. She tried his number, but that just went straight to voicemail, too. It's seemed as though no one wanted to talk to her today.

~ ~ ~

Autumn grinned at Carter. "Thank you!"

He smiled and nodded. He couldn't believe just how well this whole thing was working out. "Thank you, for not being mad at me. For a while there I was scared I was just making everything worse."

Autumn nodded. "If you'd asked me if you should do this, I would have told you hell no! It wasn't worth the risk, but I'm so glad you took the risk." She grinned. "And even more glad it paid off so well."

Clay took his headphones out and smiled over at them. "You did good, Carter. It seems to me that we all owe you one after this."

"No one owes me anything. I'm just glad it's all worked out."

Clay looked out the plane window. "Well, we're almost there, so now you get to see if the most important part of all works out."

Carter nodded. He was pretty sure it would. His head was still spinning from everything that had happened in the last twenty-four hours, but all that mattered now was getting back to Summer.

After the show last night, they'd gone to the airport and flown back to Nashville in Clay's jet. This morning, they'd gone to McAdam Records where Clay had met with both Ashley and Autumn. After that, the three of them had headed back to the airport and now they were about to land back in Bozeman. Carter had been a little surprised that both Clay and Autumn had wanted to come with him to see Summer, but he could hardly say no, could he?

Once they landed, Carter led the way to the parking lot where he'd left his truck the day before. They still had an hour's drive before he'd get to see Summer. "Do you mind if I call her before we go?"

Clay shook his head. "Let her know you're coming home, but don't spoil the surprise." He smiled at Autumn. "I want to see her face when we both show up and tell her our news."

Carter dialed her number and waited while it rang.

"Carter!" her voice didn't sound good.

"Hey, darlin', are you okay?"

"I've had better days. Where are you? When are you coming home?"

"I'm in Bozeman, I'm on my way."

"Oh, thank God. We need to talk, and I need you to stop running away from me when the going gets tough!"

"I'll try." He smiled. "I think you might be able to forgive me for this one though."

"You know I forgive you…wait, what do you mean?"

"I'll tell you when I get there."

"Okay, but hurry up, will you?"

"I'm on my way."

~ ~ ~

Summer paced the deck while she waited. It'd take him an hour to get here from Bozeman. She couldn't wait to see him, couldn't wait for him to explain what he'd meant about her being able to forgive him for having left. What had he done? She had no clue.

She tried calling her sister again while she waited, but Autumn still wasn't picking up. Summer had to hope that she was okay.

Carter stopped out on East River Road before he turned into Summer's driveway. "Can I ask a favor of you both?"

Clay and Autumn both nodded.

"Would you mind waiting in the truck a few minutes while I go see her first?"

Autumn smiled. "Of course."

Clay nodded. "I wouldn't expect anything less, son. But don't leave us out here too long, will you? You've got the rest of your life with her. I've not got long before I need to get back to the airport and on my way to Seattle."

"No problem." Carter had to hope that Clay was right and that he would get to spend the rest of his life with Summer. So many problems had been solved in the last twenty-four hours, but that didn't mean there weren't any more left. For one thing, he didn't know what Summer would do here. He didn't know what she would do anywhere if she weren't singing, but it wasn't as though there were many opportunities to do much of anything here in the valley. He started the truck back up and turned into the long driveway. One thing at a time. That was all they could deal with.

When he stopped in front of the house he said, "Won't be long," and then he jumped out of his truck. He ran up the front steps quickly, wanting to get to the front door before Summer came out and spotted his passengers. He opened the door quietly, then closed it behind him with a slam.

"Carter?" She came running out of the living room and threw herself at him. As she wrapped her arms up around his neck, he closed his own around her waist and lifted her off her feet. He lowered his head to kiss her.

She pecked his lips, but then pulled back to look at him. "Tell me what you're thinking? I was so worried. I thought you were taking off again and that you wouldn't come back."

He put a finger to her lips. Her voice sounded really bad, and she didn't need to use it up asking questions. He was about to answer them all anyway.

"I'm thinking, I love you. I'm sorry I took off without talking to you. I was just going to run, but I didn't."

"But what *did* you do?"

"I went and interfered."

She tipped her head back so she could look him in the eye. She looked worried. "You did? How?"

He grinned. "I went to see Clay."

She turned pale.

"Don't worry. It all worked out."

"But what about Ashley? What about Autumn?"

"Maybe you should talk to Autumn about that?"

"I would, but she's not answering her phone!"

Carter grinned. "Hang on a minute, then." He went back to open the front door and waved. Summer's hand flew up to cover her mouth when she saw first Autumn, then Clay climb out of the truck. She looked up at Carter with big round eyes. "What the..."

He grinned. "Like I said, I went to see Clay, we went to see Autumn, and then we all came back here. It's all going to be okay, darlin'."

She wrapped both arms around his waist and hugged him tight. He held her to him and grinned at Autumn and Clay over her head as they reached the front door. "Come on in," he said. "I think we've all got some explaining to do."

~ ~ ~

Summer was having a hard time processing it all. She'd been sitting there wondering how to convince Carter that he'd better not leave her so her sister would be okay. She'd been trying to figure out how to make sure her sister *would* be okay, no matter what Summer herself did, and she'd been wondering whether she shouldn't just risk going to Clay about it all. Now the three of them were all here, telling *her* that everything *was* okay!

Once they were all seated in the living room she looked around at them. "So what happened? What's going on?"

Clay smiled at her. "What happened is that your man here did what you should have done in the first place and came to me."

Summer nodded. She should have known Clay would take care of her—and Autumn. "I'm sorry."

"No need to be, little girl. It all worked out for the best." He grinned at Autumn. "Do you want to tell her?"

Autumn smiled. "When Carter told Clay what Ashley was doing, they both came back to Nashville. I'd set up a meeting with Ashley this morning. Like I told you yesterday, I was about to tell her I was through. In fact, I did tell her I was through."

"What did she say?"

"That she was going to make sure no one else in town would work with me."

Clay nodded. "That was the point where we walked in. I feel like a fool having given Ashley so much say over the business. I hired her believing she was the best. I was wrong—she just talks the best story. It's *her* that won't find work in Nashville again."

Wow! Summer knew what a big deal it was for Clay to fire her. Ashley had been the lynchpin of the label. It was only since she'd been around that Clay had been able to go back out on tour himself. She looked at him, hoping this wouldn't mean that he'd be tied to the office again and have his own music take a back seat. "But what will you do now?"

He grinned at Autumn. "I already knew who really was the best in the industry. Unfortunately, she was tied into an exclusive gig with one particular artist. She's free now though, and I just hired her to fill the position that became available this morning."

"Oh my God!" She looked at Autumn. "You mean you're the new Director?"

Autumn nodded. "I'd like to be. If you don't need me?"

Summer laughed. "I'll always need you—as my sister—but not as my business manager anymore." Her smile faded as she turned to Clay. "I don't want to wait until my three months are up to make the decision, Clay. I'm done." She took hold of Carter's hand. "I don't want to sing anymore. I want to stay here." She smiled up at him. "And be with the man I love."

His big brown eyes were full of love as he smiled back down at her.

"I already knew you weren't coming back, little girl. Remember what I told you before you left? When the day came you were ready to walk away, it'd be okay. It *is* okay." His expression changed. "Do you mind if I ask what you *are* going to do with yourself, though?"

Summer sighed. That was one thing that had bothered her all along. What *could* she do here? She shrugged. "I'll figure something out."

Clay raised an eyebrow. "How would you feel about writing?"

"Writing?"

He laughed. "Songs, not books! You've always written your own, how would you feel about writing for other artists?"

Summer thought about it. It could be fun. She nodded slowly.

"You don't have to decide right now, but think it over."

"I will. Thanks, Clay." He nodded, then checked his watch. "I need to get on my way. I'm in Seattle tomorrow night."

Summer looked at Autumn. "What about you?"

Autumn grinned. "I'm going with my new boss. I want to take the opportunity to bend his ear about changes I have in mind for the label. How we can do things better. And I want to..."

Clay grinned at Carter. "If I live to regret this, I'm going to be blaming you, son."

Carter grinned back at him. "You won't regret it. You wanted the best person for the job. You've got her. Now all you have to do is keep up."

Autumn got up and went to hug him. "And it's all thanks to you, Carter."

Summer loved the way he smiled. He looked proud of himself and bashful at the same time.

Clay came to shake his hand. "Thanks again, son. I'm not going to say good-bye, just see you soon, because I'm pretty sure I will."

Carter laughed. "There's not much point saying anything yet. We need to get you back to the airport. It's not as though you can just call a cab, so you've got us for another hour at least."

"Ah, good point," said Clay. "I guess I'm just used to walking outside and being able to get a cab."

"That's too much city living for you," said Carter. "You need to spend some time out here. Remember where you came from."

Summer smiled as she watched the two men together. She hoped they might become friends; they certainly seemed to have gotten off on a good foot.

Chapter Twenty-Three

It was dark by the time they got home. They'd taken Autumn
and Clay to the airport, then stopped in town for dinner on the
way back. Hero greeted them at the door when Summer
opened it.

"She's made herself right at home here, hasn't she?" Carter
said.

Summer's smile faded. "Well, she'd better not get used to it."

"Why?" Carter was shocked. He'd thought Summer loved
having her and the kittens here.

"Oh, I don't mind her at all, but it looks as though we'll have
to move."

"And why's that?"

"I'm so upset with Beau! With everything that's happened
today I didn't get a chance to tell you about it, but apparently
he's had an offer he can't refuse on the house."

"Ah."

She looked at him. "I've always stood up for him and said he's
not as bad as people make out, but I'm really disappointed in
him right now."

Carter felt bad. "Don't be too hard on him. You don't know
the full story yet."

"I suppose, but I do know he said I could have first refusal, and now he's changed his mind."

Carter nodded. He didn't want to get into it just yet. He came to stand behind her and wrapped his arms around her waist. "How about we get a glass of wine and go sit in the hot tub? That should help you relax."

She twisted around in his arms to smile up at him. "That sounds perfect. And while we drink our wine and watch the stars, we can figure out where we go from here. Not just about a house, but..." she searched his face. "You know, everything."

He did know. He wanted the two of them to decide where they went from here. Well, he knew where he wanted to go. He just had to ask her. He was hoping with all his being that she was going to say yes.

He handed her a glass of wine then stepped into the hot tub and sat down beside her. She looked so beautiful out here under the stars. They'd left the jets off so they could listen to the sounds of the river and the night. The moonlight reflected off the water and danced in her eyes as she smiled at him. "I love you, Carter," she said.

He smiled. "And I love you, Summer. More than you know."

She put her hand on his leg and squeezed his thigh, sending ripples of desire coursing through him. "Want to show me how much?" she asked with a wicked smile.

He did, but not just yet. "I'll show you, all night long," he said. He wrapped an arm around her shoulders and drew her closer. "There are a couple of things I want to ask you first."

She looked so earnest as she looked up at him. "What?"

He drew in a deep breath. For a second he lost his nerve, so he went with the easier question first. "Do you really love this house?"

She shrugged. "I do, but I don't see that it matters, since Beau is selling it out from under me."

"But he's not. What exactly did he say?"

She thought about it. "He said that he'd had an offer he couldn't refuse."

"He couldn't refuse it, because I'm his brother and I asked him not to."

She looked confused. "Why would you do that?"

"Because it was me that made the offer. I want to buy it."

"Oh!" She might not have the words, but her eyes and her smile expressed just how happy she was. "But you don't need to. I was going to."

"I know, but it's important to me. I want to be the one to buy our home." It *was* important. He knew that she had much more money than he did, but it mattered to him. Although he'd said he'd love to live here with her, he didn't love the idea of living off her. He knew it wasn't like that really, but he couldn't help it. It was how he saw himself as a man, and he wanted to able to provide a home for her.

She leaned her head on his arm and smiled up at him. "Do you think maybe we could do what normal couples do and buy it between us?"

He thought about that, and smiled. He liked it. That would mean they were in it together, equals, partners. He nodded slowly. It was time to ask his other question. "So you want to be my partner?"

She looked puzzled. He was messing this up. "You mean in the house?"

"I mean in life."

She cocked her head to one side.

He had to just come out and say it. He slid off the seat and knelt in the bottom of the hot tub. It wasn't exactly down on one knee, but it was as close as he was going to get with warm water swirling around his chest. "I mean in life, Summer. I'm making a big old mess of this, but what I'm trying to say is…" he placed his hands on either side of her legs and looked up into her eyes, knowing that his whole future was riding on the next few words. "Summer, I love you. I want to spend the rest of my life showing you how much. Will you marry me?"

Tears filled her eyes as she grasped his shoulders and nodded. "Yes! Oh, Carter, yes! I'd love to marry you!" She sank her fingers in his hair and pulled him closer to kiss him.

He closed his arms around her and pulled her down into the water to join him. This was the happiest night of his life. He loved this woman with all his heart and soul, and she'd just agreed to marry him! He kissed her deeply and tenderly, wanting to make the moment last, knowing this was a memory that would etch itself into his mind and his heart forever.

When they finally came up for air she smiled at him and wrapped her arms around his neck. "I love you, Carter Remington."

"And I love you, Summer Breese." He chuckled. "You don't need to change your name if you don't want to."

"And why's that?"

"I like your name. It sums you up. You're all warm and sunny and a breath of fresh air."

"You're quite the romantic when you want to be."

He shrugged. He wasn't trying to be romantic; he wouldn't know how. He was just telling her what he thought. That was all. Then it hit him. He really was a dumbass, not a romantic at all. He'd asked her to marry him and completely forgotten about the important bit. The bit women liked and thought was romantic. He stood up sending a wave washing over the side of the hot tub.

Summer stood, too, with a grin. "Now you're going to show me how much you love me?" she asked as she ran her eyes over him appreciatively.

He chuckled and shook his head. He loved that she couldn't get enough of him and that she wasn't afraid to say so. "Not just yet. There's something I need to take care of first." He climbed out of the hot tub and helped her out too. Wrapping towels around them, he led her back into the house and into the bedroom. He opened up the holdall he'd taken with him when he left yesterday. He hadn't had much time in Nashville this morning, but while Autumn had gone home to pack a bag, he'd asked Clay to take him to a jeweler's shop. He'd also asked Clay to help him pick. He had no clue what Summer might like. But Clay had told him to go with his gut and he had.

He sat down on the bed and held the little box up to Summer. "Go on, open it."

She smiled down at him then carefully opened the box. "Oh, Carter it's beautiful!" She really meant it. He could tell by the way her eyes shone.

He took the ring out of the box and slid it onto her finger. "I can change it if you don't like it."

She shook her head rapidly. "Don't you dare! I love it. It's beautiful." She held her hand up to admire it then put both hands on his shoulders and pushed him back onto the bed. He lay back and smiled up at her as she climbed on and sat astride him.

"Is a wife allowed to ride her husband?"

He nodded eagerly. "She's not just allowed to; it's highly recommended."

"I'm glad to hear it." She smiled and let her towel fall away.

Carter's hands reached up with a will of their own and closed around her breasts making her sigh and writhe on top of him.

Her hands closed around him, drawing a sigh of his own as she guided him to her. He was lost and he knew it. This little lady didn't just hold his cock in her hands; she held his future, his happiness, his whole life. He closed his eyes as she slowly impaled herself on him. He thrust his hips and dropped his hands to her waist as he began to move beneath her. She was his. She rode him hard and he gladly went with her, his hips bucking, claiming her with every thrust. Her breath grew shallow and he knew she was close. He let himself go taking her with him as she cried his name. He saw stars as he gave her all that he was, and she took it while she gave herself to him. When she finally slumped down onto his chest he wrapped an arm around her and stroked her hair.

He was the luckiest man alive. She was his woman, she was going to be his wife, and he loved her with all his heart.

"I'm going to marry you," she mumbled.

He chuckled. "You better had now, you took the ring."

She pushed herself up on her elbows and smiled down at him. "I knew you were special on the day we met, but who would have thought we'd end up here?"

His heart swelled with happiness. "I think I fell in love with you that day."

She raised an eyebrow. "Really?"

He nodded. "Yeah. I mean, sure, you were the country singer, the dream girl I'd fantasized about, but I would never have expected that to translate into reality. But then I met you and you were so much more than I thought you were. I spent a long time trying to tell myself it wasn't love, but deep inside I knew."

"How did you know?"

He shrugged. "The heart wants what it wants, and when it finds it, it knows."

She dropped a kiss onto his lips. "You really are a romantic at heart, aren't you?"

He closed his arms around her. "If you say so, darlin'." He rolled her onto her side. "I guess it's not too romantic that I need to get in the shower after that hot tub though is it?"

She grinned. "It could be. If you take me with you."

"I think the word is insatiable—not romantic—and that'd be you. Not me."

~ ~ ~

Summer held Carter's hand as they walked up to the big house. He'd called around and asked everyone to meet them at the ranch. She smiled up at him. "What do you think your parents will say?"

"Honestly?"

That made her nervous. She was pretty sure his brothers would be happy for them. She hoped his parents would, too, but considering what he'd been through in the past, she'd understand if they were wary.

He wrapped his arm around her shoulders. "Don't look so scared. What I honestly think they'll say is, told you so!"

She laughed in relief. "Really?"

He nodded. "Remember that night you came to dinner with everyone?"

"Yes."

"I told them you wouldn't be here for long and I asked them to help me pick up the pieces when you left."

Summer's heart melted for him. He was such a big strong guy, but he wasn't afraid to admit his vulnerability.

"My mom told me then that I was wrong. I wanted to believe her, but I didn't dare."

Summer smiled. "I'm so glad she was right."

He nodded. "Not as glad as I am."

When they walked into the kitchen the others were already there. Summer met Monique's gaze and smiled. The older woman smiled back then quickly shot a look at Summer's left hand. She looked back up with the biggest smile on her face. Summer let go of Carter's hand and went to her. The two women hugged each other tight. "I won't ever hurt him," whispered Summer. She wanted Monique to understand.

"I know." Tears shone in her eyes.

"What's all that about?" asked Shane with a grin.

Summer turned back to Carter. She wanted him to have this moment. To tell his family and share their happiness with all of them.

She went to him and slipped under his arm, sliding her own around his waist as she smiled around at everyone.

"I think you can all probably guess, but we wanted to come tell you officially."

"Tell us what?" asked his dad with a big grin on his face.

"That Summer has agreed to do me the honor of becoming my wife."

Summer got lost in all the hugging and backslapping and congratulating. Beau came to hug her and gave her an apologetic smile. "I hope you're not mad at me now that you understand?"

She shook her head and hugged him back. "Not at all."

She loved this family. She loved that they loved each other so much and saw each other through the ups and the downs. She turned to find Carter, he was watching her with a big smile on his face and love shining out of his big brown eyes. Most of all she loved this man. Her man. Carter;

A Note from SJ

I hope you enjoyed your visit to Montana and spending time with the Remingtons. Please let your friends know about the books if you feel they would enjoy them as well. It would be wonderful if you would leave me a review, I'd very much appreciate it.

You can check out the rest of the series on my website www.SJMcCoy.com to keep up with the brothers as they each find their happiness.

Chance has finally talked me into giving him his own three book spin-off. Look out for it in Spring 2017.

In the meantime, you'll see glimpses of him in my Summer Lake series, too. If you haven't read them, you can get started with Emma and Jack in Book One, Love Like You've Never Been Hurt which is currently FREE to download in ebook form from all the big online book retailers AND early in 2017 the whole series will be available in paperback as well!

There are a few options to keep up with me and my imaginary friends:

The best way is to Sign up on the website for my Newsletter. Don't worry I won't bombard you! I'll let you know about upcoming releases, share a sneak peek or two and keep you in the loop for a couple of fun giveaways I have coming up :0)

You can join my readers group to chat about the books on Facebook or just browse and like my Facebook Page

I occasionally attempt to say something in 140 characters or less(!) on Twitter

And I'm always in the process of updating my website at www.SJMcCoy.com with new book updates and even some videos. Plus, you'll find the latest news on new releases and giveaways in my blog.

I love to hear from readers, so feel free to email me at AuthorSJMcCoy@gmail.com.. I'm better at that! :0)

I hope our paths will cross again soon. Until then, take care, and thanks for your support—you are the reason I write!
Love
SJ

PS Project Semicolon

You may have noticed that the final sentence of the story closed with a semi-colon. It isn't a typo. <u>Project Semi Colon</u> is a non-profit movement dedicated to presenting hope and love to those who are struggling with depression, suicide, addiction and self-injury. Project Semicolon exists to encourage, love and inspire. It's a movement I support with all my heart.

"A semicolon represents a sentence the author could have ended, but chose not to. The sentence is your life and the author is you."

    - Project Semicolon

This author started writing after her son was killed in a car crash. At the time, I wanted my own story to be over, instead I chose to honour a promise to my son to write my 'silly stories' someday. I chose to escape into my fictional world. I know for many who struggle with depression, suicide can appear to be the only escape. The semicolon has become a symbol of support, and hopefully a reminder – Your story isn't over yet

Also by SJ McCoy

Remington Ranch Series
Mason (FREE in ebook form)
Shane
Carter
Beau

Coming next
Four Weddings and a Vendetta

Summer Lake Series
Love Like You've Never Been Hurt (FREE in ebook form)
Work Like You Don't Need the Money
Dance Like Nobody's Watching
Fly Like You've Never Been Grounded
Laugh Like You've Never Cried
Sing Like Nobody's Listening
Smile Like You Mean It
The Wedding Dance
Chasing Tomorrow
Dream Like Nothing's Impossible

Coming next
Ride Like You've Never Fallen

About the Author

I'm SJ, a coffee addict, lover of chocolate and drinker of good red wines. I'm a lost soul and a hopeless romantic. Reading and writing are necessary parts of who I am. Though perhaps not as necessary as coffee! I can drink coffee without writing, but I can't write without coffee.

I grew up loving romance novels, my first boyfriends were book boyfriends, but life intervened, as it tends to do, and I wandered down the paths of non-fiction for many years. My life changed completely a few years ago and I returned to Romance to find my escape.

I write 'Sweet n Steamy' stories because to me there is enough angst and darkness in real life. My favorite romances are happy escapes with a focus on fun, friendships and happily-ever-afters, just like the ones I write.

These days I live in beautiful Montana, the last best place. If I'm not reading or writing, you'll find me just down the road in the park - Yellowstone. I have deer, eagles and the occasional bear for company, and I like it that way :0)

Made in the USA
Lexington, KY
09 January 2017